"OH, YES, I WANT TO GO HOME"

*To Chuck & Bev —
The title of this book
isn't really accurate —
we don't want to
go home!
John Wils[?]
Feb, '97*

"OH, YES, I WANT TO GO HOME"

A Novel About the American Civil War

By
John M. Wilson

Original Art Work and Book Layout By
Ric A. Wilson

All photographs from the 1861-1865 Period

Published By:
Paint Rock Publishing, Inc.
Kingston, Tennessee

1996

Copyright 1995 by John M. Wilson
Paint Rock Publishing, Inc.

All rights reserved. No part of this publication may be reproduced or transmitted in any form or by any means, electronic or mechanical, including photocopy, recording, or any information storage and retrieval system, without permission in writing from the publisher.

Requests for permission to make copies of any part of the work should be mailed to:
Permissions
Paint Rock Publishing, Inc.
118 Dupont Smith Lane
Kingston, Tennessee 37763
(423) 376-3892

Publisher's Cataloging in Publication
(Prepared by Quality Books, Inc.)

Wilson, John Morris, 1939-
  "Oh, Yes, I Want To Go Home" ; a novel about the American Civil War / by John M. Wilson.
  p. cm.
  Includes bibliographical references.
  ISBN 0-9649394-0-1

  1. United States--History--Civil War, 1861-1865--Fiction. I. Title.

PS3573.I5766O49 1996   813'.54
                         QBI96-20041

Manufactured in the United States of America
First Edition

"OH, YES, I WANT TO GO HOME"

I WANT TO GO HOME

"Dere's no rain to wet you,
O, yes, I want to go home.

Dere's no sun to burn you,
O, yes, I want to go home

O, push along, believers,
O, yes, I want to go home

Dere's no hard trials,
O, yes, I want to go home

Dere's no whips a---crackin',
O, yes, I want to go home

My brudder on de wayside,
O, yes, I want to go home

O, push along, my brudder,
O, yes, I want to go home

Where dere's no stormy weather,
O, yes, I want to go home

Dere's no tribulation,
O, yes, I want to go home"

Negro Spiritual from "Army Life in a Black Regiment"
by Thomas Wentworth Higginson
1870, Fields, Osgood, & Co., Boston, Massachusetts

PREFACE

This book is a following of three imaginary brothers, slaves on a South Carolina plantation, through the four years of the American Civil War, 1861-1865. No resemblance to any person in our historical past or our present is intended.

The germ of an idea for this book came while I was researching and writing a book, *I Have Looked Death in the Face: The Civil War Career of William Porcher DuBose*. That book is a biography of Dr. DuBose, an officer in the Confederate Army with the Holcombe Legion of South Carolina, who became a chaplain with Kershaw's Brigade in 1863, and served through the remainder of the war in that capacity. Following the war, he became chaplain and professor of theology at the University of the South in Sewanee, Tennessee, and one of the foremost theologians in the Episcopal Church. In preparing for that book, I learned that Dr. DuBose, son of a wealthy South Carolina plantation owner, had with him for the length of the war, a body servant, one of the slaves from his father's plantation.

The research into Dr. DuBose's life intrigued me so much that I began reading a number of books about how blacks in the South were able to survive the war and what they were likely to have done during those tumultuous four years. A male black American in 1861-1865 had basically three principal routes, in general not of his choosing. They were as follows:

• To assist the South in the war effort. The first possibility was to remain on the plantation as he always had, working in fields or house, freeing up white Southerners for participation in the war as soldiers. The second possibility that aided the Southern cause was to be rented or sold to Confederate authorities, usually to be used as workers on defense works around cities, such as breastworks, forts, etc. The slave who went this route was thought to be in worse shape than those who remained on the plantation; rations and health care were in general not even as good as they were at home.

- To run at the first opportunity. He could have attached himself to the nearest Northern Army, where he was either impressed into service or became a soldier at the earliest time possible. The Union did not form many black regiments until relatively late in the war, but there were early units, such as the First South Carolina Volunteers (Fus Souf, in the vernacular) which were formed on the Sea Islands on the South Carolina coast as early as 1861. He could also have run North, where as an impressed worker, he was not much better off than he was on the plantation. Many were promised wages, but all were not paid.

- To be assigned as a body servant to a Confederate officer. These servants became very loyal, particularly those who were chosen from slaves on the plantation. Those hired were generally not so loyal. There are numerous accounts of home chosen servants who, when they had an opportunity to escape, refused to do so. These servants became the elite of the slave population, and many became involved in the war effort in various ways For many decades following the war, black body servants attended Confederate reunions, and some states (albeit after many years) actually gave body servants Confederate pensions.

The premise of this novel is to follow three brothers, Nathan, James and Stephen, from 1861 through 1865, on the paths that fate chose for them. The intent is to be historically accurate as possible. In the process of writing, I read and researched a number of books, some specifically on the fate of blacks during and after the war. Some contained information germane to my story. I have included a bibliography containing references to many of these books. Preceding the bibliography is a glossary containing cross-references of words used in the vernacular by Southern blacks during this period. I have chosen the literary approach of having black characters think and talk to themselves in contemporary language, to make reading easier.

I have used the name of the Holcombe Legion, South Carolina Volunteers, as the unit to which "Young Master Will" and his body servant, Nathan, were attached because of my familiarity with the activities of that unit during the American Civil War. The locations of battles in which Will and Nathan participated are roughly the same as theaters in which the Holcombe Legion actually fought.

Overall, my intent is to present that which "could have happened", and, at the same time, not to stray too far afield.

Finally, my thanks go to those who aided me in preparation of this book. The following persons critically read the manuscript and made valuable suggestions which made the book substantially more readable: C.W. Wilson, III, Ross A. Haeberle, and Ms. Brenda Altom. Ms. Julia Field Goodwin did a superb job of final edit and review, but any errors are those of the writer alone. Ms. Benita Ferrell took my rough manuscript and made it far more presentable. Mr. Ric A. Wilson assisted in many ways in the production of this book, including preparation of the original black and white sketches which grace these pages. He also helped in set up and preparation of camera-ready copy of the manuscript and designed the cover.

John M. Wilson
Kingston, Tennessee
1996

PHOTOGRAPH CREDITS

Massachusetts Commandery Military Order Of The Loyal Legion/U.S. Army Military History Institute
(Pages 18, 32, 76, 102, 130, 158, 170, 216, Cover)

United States National Archives
(Pages 42, 56, 86, 94, 117, 136, 137, 142, 143, 159, 171, 182, 196, 197, 208, 209, Frontispiece)

United States Library of Congress
(Pages 87, 95, 116, 183, 217)

TABLE OF CONTENTS

PROLOGUE 14
CHAPTER ONE - THE STATUS QUO 19
CHAPTER TWO - THE SOUNDS OF WAR 33
CHAPTER THREE - THE BEGINNING 43
CHAPTER FOUR - OFF TO WAR,
THEN THERE WERE TWO 57
CHAPTER FIVE - THE HOME FOLKS' WAR 77
CHAPTER SIX - FLIGHT 87
CHAPTER SEVEN - THEN THERE WAS ONE 95
CHAPTER EIGHT - THE FLIGHT CONTINUES 103
CHAPTER NINE - THE WAR IN
NORTHERN VIRGINIA 117
CHAPTER TEN - BACK ON THE HOMEPLACE 131
CHAPTER ELEVEN - AND THE
MARCHING WENT ON, AND ON, AND ON 137
CHAPTER TWELVE - THE MARYLAND CAMPAIGN .. 143
CHAPTER THIRTEEN - KEEP THE
HOME FIRES BURNING 159
CHAPTER FOURTEEN - THE PACE INCREASES 171
CHAPTER FIFTEEN - ANOTHER SPRING..................... 183
CHAPTER SIXTEEN - THE HOME
FRONT GETS TOUGHER.. 197
CHAPTER SEVENTEEN - THE LAST LEGS................... 209
CHAPTER EIGHTEEN - HOME, SWEET(?), HOME ... 217
GLOSSARY 226
BIBLIOGRAPHY 231

PROLOGUE

The August evening was balmy, and a soft breeze brought welcome moisture as it crossed the river. Nat felt its cool presence as he leaned on the split rail fence on the river bank. He reflected on the day's work and felt satisfaction recalling all that had been accomplished. As he mused on pleasant thoughts, unwanted violent memories complete with sight and sound thrust themselves into the forefront of his mind.

Even though the war had been over for these thirty years, Nat still saw cameos of scenes he had tried to forget. Most vivid was the hell which followed every battle, after the cannon ceased its ground-shaking roar and the staccato chatter of small arms fire ended. The hell included sounds of suffering. Shrieks of innocent horses ridden by men or transporting their infernal machines of killing and destruction. Cries of wounded men, limb-shot and knowing they faced a surgeon's knife and stood a better chance of dying there than in the battle. If gut-shot, they faced a long, painful death. So certain was their death, the litter bearers didn't pick them up until all other wounded were collected.

The carnage of the War Between the States is hard to imagine and was equally hard for participants to forget. Armament had outstripped maneuvering—the ones who paid for this disparity were flesh-and-bone soldiers. Nat reflected on the many times when he and the other body servants attached to the Holcombe Legion crept out onto the battlefield to carry water to the wounded, providing a measure of relief to Gray and Blue—it didn't matter which color—the agony was still the same.

Nat stood upright and shook his graying head. It was now 1895, and pleasurable events were about to happen. He hoped and prayed good times would push the painful memories further into the dark and dusty recesses of his mind. His eldest daughter was to be married the next day, and Nat's former owner and master Will, now his employer and friend, was coming to enjoy the wedding and festivities to follow. Nat "killed the fatted calf" for this celebration and looked forward to the happenings. His brother Stephen and family planned to cross the field from his house to join in.

Nat had a fleeting thought: I wish Momma was alive to enjoy tomorrow.

Nat shook his head again, no more sad thoughts. Times had not been all bad from 1861-1895, the time of several revolutions fought so that today Nathan could stand on his land and answer only to his Maker, not to a master or slave overseer. Thus, the revolutions were on the whole, a good thing. Nat could not even conjure what life might be if that war had not been fought. He shook his head again. The war was fought, my children and I are free, and most white men in the county treat us as equals, except for a few trash. Nat reckoned that there was trash of every color, and he couldn't worry about them.

With these thoughts still spinning through his head, he walked towards the house, where the soft beams of yellow light streamed out of the windows and beckoned him to wrap himself in their warmth and protection and to relax. Nat thought, I'm glad the relaxing time of the day is here, and maybe memories of the days of killing will stay away tonight, and I can dream about only happy things—past, present, and future.

☐ ☐ ☐ ☐

"OH, YES, I WANT TO GO HOME"

CHAPTER ONE
THE STATUS QUO
The Brothers
Spring, 1861

Nathan's black skin shone like burnished ebony with beads of sweat popping out of every pore. It was an unbelievably, unbearably hot, muggy day. Not just hot, thought Nathan as he painfully stood up and rubbed the palms of his hands against the aching small of his back. Maybe the hottest day he could remember this early in cotton-picking season. He shuffled his bare feet in the rich soil of South Carolina's Coastal Plain. He felt substantially older than his nineteen years. The sweat rolled down his face and into his eyes and stung them, and he mopped his face with the old dirty rag which he had stuffed in the rope that held up his pants. The weather always looked to be worse when it came time to spend dawn-to-dusk in the fields to bring in the crop which supported the plantation where Nathan lived and worked.

Nathan looked across the seemingly endless field of cotton and saw the shimmering heat waves which made the field look as if it were on fire. On the other side of the cotton rows, forests of palmetto trees were too far away to provide any shade; it was entirely too early in the day to consider how cool shade might feel. Even the starkly contrasting colors of the bright green cotton plants, the rich black South Carolina soil, and the bright blue sky with white clouds failed to cheer Nathan.

Nathan looked over at the next row, where his brothers, James and Stephen, slowly and methodically stripped white cotton pods off the waist-high plants and dropped them into the bags slung across their shoulders. At 16, James was the youngest, while Stephen at 17 was two years younger than Nathan. Nathan was a good-looking lad, one to whom the girls paid a great deal of attention during church services every Sunday. Nathan had received a few thumps on his head from Momma when he squirmed in an attempt to get more attention from the girls. Retribution from Momma was generally swift and painful.

Nathan was suddenly jerked back into the present by a gruff voice that shouted almost in his ear, "Hey, niggah! Goin tuh stand there all day dreamin, or are you goin tuh do your share? You heard Master Richard say before he left that he expected you worthless slaves tuh finish these rows today, or there would be no food tonight for you!" Nathan turned and looked directly into the face of the white overseer for the plantation.

"Yassuh," responded Nathan, "I wuz jes restin my back. You know I always pick as much cotton as anybuddy!"

The overseer said in a low, threatening voice at odds with his slender build, "Don't smart at me, or I'll give you a taste of this whip. Now, get back tuh work. Bend your back, niggah, or I'll bend it for you. Git movin!"

"Yassuh," said Nathan, and he bent back to the mindless, endless task at hand. He shut down his mind and the responses he dared not venture. He resumed the rhythm needed to survive days of this labor.

He thought to himself, I sure wish that Massuh Richard hadn't seen fit to hire Ely, the new overseer. The old one, who had suddenly left the Low Country in South Carolina where the plantation was located, had been bad enough. Nathan talked with slaves on the next plantation during a trip that Master Will, son of the plantation owner, had recently taken to visit the pretty daughters of the neighbor. Nathan rode the old brown and white mottled plow mule along side of Master Will and was able to spend some time with the neighboring slaves to catch up on gossip. Those slaves had told him that Ely was known as a bad overseer at the farm upcountry where he used to work. He was known for his use of the blacksnake whip much too often on the slaves--a way to "keep them respectful"-- which Master Richard had never seemed to require.

Nathan recalled that once years ago when he was only five or six years old, Master Richard had run off an overseer for too liberal use of the whip, which left hideous scars on the backs and legs of slaves, reducing their value. Numerous scars on a slave indicated that man or woman was rebellious and had to be watched constantly.

Nathan thought to himself, Boy, you think way too much. Let your mind run free, and stop making it so hard on yourself. Thinking and picking cotton at the same time is one job too many. I wish I could make little brother James feel that way, too. He's beginning to worry me with his questioning all the time about our life and why we have to be slaves, and asking why anyone has the right to own another human being, like plantation livestock. He's young and in a real rebellious mood, and that can be nothing but trouble for him and all of us.

I think James's mood really started when Poppa died, back a few months ago. We'd all seen it coming, what with Poppa getting thinner all the time, the worry-lines on his face getting deeper, and his hair growing whiter every day. Master Richard saw it too, and even sent down the white folks' doctor to see about Poppa, but he said that there was nothing he could do.

James really took it hard when Poppa went, and Ely made us go back to the fields the same day we buried Poppa, without even a chance for us to properly grieve. If Master Richard hadn't been gone up to Columbia to see the bankers, he would have let us grieve, I reckon! But, he was gone, the overseer sent us out, and James sure took it hard. If he don't get himself straight, Master Richard will sell him for sure, and I don't want that to happen!

I saw what happened at the next plantation when the white folks sold some of their slaves. It split up several families! Those people took it mighty hard, and there are those who say that old Auntie Mae died of a broken heart when they sold away her youngest daughter. I want to stay with James and Stephen, even though sometimes we don't get along, fighting and carrying on, but we all love each other. It's hardest on me, oldest of the three of us, trying to help Momma with Poppa so recent gone.

Nathan was interrupted in his reveries by the melodious sounds of the ringing of the old wagon wheel band which Master Richard had long ago hung in the tree by the Big House. He looked up and found to his surprise that dusk had suddenly crept up on them, and the palmetto trees were not even visible in deepening shadows across the cotton field. One more day in the dreary, monotonous life of a slave on a South Carolina plantation in 1861, had painfully ground to a close. He picked up his last bag of cotton, and alongside James and Stephen in the darkening evening, slowly trudged back toward the collection of small, rickety, wooden-sided shacks in the slave quarters. On the way back, he again tried to warn James of what was going to happen if he didn't quit sassing the overseer or making faces at him behind his back.

As soon as Nathan started to speak his piece and James realized the direction he was going, James reacted as he normally did—he told Nathan to shut up.

James said, "I'm tired o hearin bout dat stuff! You ain't my Poppa, and I don't hab tuh listen tuh you. Now jes shut dat mouf o yours afore I shuts it fer you. You mite be older but I spec I kin whup you if need be!"

Stephen, short and stocky and the slowest of the three who always seemed to listen and seldom to talk, sadly shook his head and added, "I hates it when you two fuss and carry on lik dat. You make my head hurt, for shore."

Nathan glanced at James and nodded. "All right, little brudder, I'll stop a-warnin fer now. But I gots tuh say whut I gots tuh say. Sumbody gots to keep dis hothead outa trubble!"

"Not tuh me you don't gots tuh say anythin," growled James. "Not tuh me!" Nathan practically bit his tongue to keep from saying anything else, but vowed to himself this debate wasn't finished or done with. He fully aimed to do what Poppa would have done and keep James out of trouble, in spite of himself!

Without further trouble and with no more words, the boys completed their half-mile walk and arrived at the edge of the clearing where they shared the clap boarded slave-quarter cabin with Momma. In the distance, they could hear the happy sounds of the youngest slave children at play; James felt that, somehow, that sound was out of place with their status in life. Those children would learn soon enough that there would be little for them to laugh at later as they grew into "workin size."

The brothers arrived at the small rock spring-house which furnished the water they had to carry to the cabin every day to wash and cook with; they all stopped at the spring overflow to wash their faces and hands of the day's accumulation of South Carolina soil mixed with their own sweat. Momma always insisted that they come to dinner with clean hands and faces.

As was the custom on their plantation, the "meal-preparer" for the family was allowed to depart the fields about an hour before the other field workers. Most days, the boys were happy with this, because it meant Momma had supper on or very near the table. James might sound off at Nathan on a regular basis, but he was smart enough to do what Momma said. With a pained and chagrined look on his face, Nathan remembered the many thumps on his woolly head it took to drum that lesson into him.

As they came into the center of the sand-floored clearing in the palmettos where the cabins were located, they saw white-haired Ned, the unofficial leader within the slaves' community, and the three stopped for just a minute to talk to him.

Ned excitedly asked them, "Hab you he—he—he—ard why Mass-ss-a went tuh Charleston? One ob th—e—e—e house boys telled me tha—a—at all ob de white folks from de Low Coun—t—t—ry wuz thar, and th—th—dey cided th—th—dat Souf Carolina is its own count—t—try!"

"What's you talkin bout, Ned?" asked James. "Everbuddy knows Souf Carolina is in de United States, not its own country. Youz dizzy in yore head!"

"It's tr—tr—true," said Ned. "He telled me dat Massuh wuz ex—ex—excited and t—t—talked bout it all de way h—h—h—ome. He said he spected a war—r—r!"

"I ain't got time tuh listen tuh old men's babblin—supper's waitin," said James. "Let's gwine eat! Ned, when you kin talk sense, come see us. Not till den!"

The boys picked up their pace and ran through the clearing. They hurried into the cabin just as Momma was beginning to get that thundercloud look that she got when she was aiming to dish out thumps rather than beans. None of the boys wanted that!

The boys entered the dimly lit cabin where they had lived all their lives. Nathan paused for just a moment to look around the interior, as if he had never before seen it. He could see the vestiges of the sunset filtering through cracks in the wallboards, and the light reflected back on smoke generated by the cook stove where Momma presided. The inside of the boards appeared almost as weathered as the exterior, and he saw the pallets set up in different corners of the cabin. Momma's corner had an old comforter hung up as a wall or door. As oldest child, he had his own corner where his covers were neatly laid out on his pallet on the floor.

James and Stephen shared a corner, and Nathan noticed that their pallets were not so neatly arranged. Momma would probably nag them about that, sooner or later. The old oil lamp flickered where it hung in the center of the cabin, suspended from the rafters, and it took Nathan's eyes a minute or two to adjust. Not much, but home sweet home. Nathan could hardly imagine living in any other circumstances as this was the only life and home he had ever known.

The first part of supper went along with only the sounds of the buzzing flies and the chewing jaws, as the boys, slumped over and tired from their exhausting day, satiated their bellies' hunger. Nathan was in the process of wiping up the last bean juice with a scrap of cornpone, thinking that they had passed a meal with no fussing.

James suddenly burst out, "I jes don't understand why we'uns hab tuh be slaves! Joseph says dat thar are lots ob cullud folks up in the North Country who ain't slaves, and dey ebben hab real jobs and dey own dey own houses!"

Momma exclaimed, "You needs tuh spend less time wit dat nocount nigger Joseph! He ain't nothing but trubble awaitin tuh happen! You keeps talkin wid him an de two ob you am gwine be sold to some oder place where you git whupped regular. I jes as soon keeps you here, but I spec my life would be easier iffn you am gone."

"Aw, Momma, you jest don't like Joseph cause he tinks for hisself an say whut am on his mind, sted of worryin bout how Massuh want him to tink an speak," responded James.

"Boy, you git on up from dis here table if'n you gwine talk tuh yore Momma lik dat!"

James stood up and pushed his chair back with such violence that it crashed on the floor. He didn't even stop to pick it up, risking a later confrontation with Momma. Instead, he rushed out of the door and across the clearing to find his friend Joseph. These evening discussion sessions were a regular pastime, even though he knew they were making him more and more unhappy with his situation in life—the same as that of some three million other slaves in the Southern United States in 1861. However, in this case, the old "misery loves company" didn't pacify or heal the deep, bitter feelings that James was experiencing.

James crossed the clearing and moved into the shadow of the palmetto grove which surrounded the slave quarters. There he found Joseph, who waited for him seated on one of the fallen logs in the grove. Both James and Joseph were eager to talk about what each of them had heard that day. The grapevine on the plantation was alive and well.

"James, I heared dat de Northern States haz elected a president dat is agin us bein slaves, and he aims tuh set us free!"

"Gwine long wit you, you been listening tuh dat fuzzy-headed ole man Ned," responded James in a disgusted tone of voice. "We heared de same ting from him comin back from de fields."

"No, itz true! I don't hear it from Ned—I heared it from a house boy dat don't lie!"

James said, "It don't make no difference. Massuh and de oder white plantation bosses ain't nebber gwine let us go. Who'd pick their cotton and make all dat money dat keeps dem rich?"

Joseph retorted, "It don't matter what dey thinks--iffin President Lincum says dey has tuh do it, dey has tuh do it!"

James and Joseph sat with their heads together for several hours past dark, talking this exhilarating freedom talk until James felt his head spinning. He realized that freedom or no freedom, if he didn't soon go back home and sleep, the next day of picking cotton in the South Carolina heat would truly be unbearable.

James returned home, where he found three pairs of completely deaf ears turned away from his excited babbling. He went to bed on the pallet with his head ringing, and he had a terrible time making himself sleep. He faced the wall and tried to imagine living elsewhere under totally different circumstances—a free man. It took all of his skills in imagining, but he finally succeeded and sleep came.

Way before dawn, James awoke with a start, when Momma planted a foot in his ribs to wake him. His mind was still working on the discussion with Joseph. He sat quietly eating his breakfast, his mind too busy to enjoy the leftover cornbread with a little bacon added in. He left with Nathan and Stephen for the far field.

That day, Momma was working with some of the other women slaves in a closer field, where they were removing stubble left over from an earlier planting.

Once the boys reached the far field, the repetition of cotton picking tasks calmed James down for a while. In fact, he picked more than his share of cotton during the morning. For some reason, he achieved the rhythm of picking easier than usual.

It was in the afternoon that the trouble began. The hot Carolina sun baked sense out of his head as well as strength out of his body. It started when Ely singled James out for special attention. Attention was something all of the slaves avoided whenever possible. This was particularly true with this overseer, as he got a special delight in harassing James.

"Hey Boy! I seen you talkin with that no count trouble makin niggah Joseph last night when I was ridin past the cabins," said Ely. "What was you niggahs discussin? You figger you kin think like a white man? You black monkeys ain't supposed tuh do nuttin but work and do what we tell you. You know you can't think!"

James remembered the warning that Nathan had been preaching at him for some time. He bit his tongue and said nothing. He hoped to avoid any confrontation by means of silence.

Ely persisted, however. "I asked you a question, niggah! You either talk tuh me, or you'll wish you had! What was it you was talkin about?"

James blurted out, "We wuz jes talkin bout de singin fore church on Sunday. Dat's all! Nuttin else, Boss!"

"Don't lie tuh me, you black son of a bitch! Do you think I'm as stupid as you are?" Ely pulled back his arm and cracked the whip in front of James's nose in a naked threat. Nathan and Stephen and all the other field hands in the vicinity stopped what they were doing and stood there with their mouths agape.

James, now terrified enough to forget Nathan's warnings and his own resolutions, gasped out the truth; "We wuz jest talking bout Massuh Lincum, dat new president de Northern folks jest elected. Bout how he wuz agin slavery."

Ely again pulled back his arm. But this time, it was no threat—when the arm came forward, the whip connected with James's back, cutting the skin and leaving an angry welt and blood trickling down his back.

As Ely took aim again Master Will rode up on his horse. Luckily for James, he came to the fields on a regular basis to find out what was going on.

"Stop that!" he yelled at Ely. "You know my father doesn't hold for whipping!"

The overseer responded, "It was jest that this black son of Satan was sayin that the new president Lincoln is agin slavery. I was tryin tuh get that nonsense out of his head afore real trouble began. We don't need these slaves a'thinkin things like that!"

"Unfortunately," said Will, "That just may be true! We don't know. It's for sure that we planters can't take that chance. The Black Republican Party is a complete unknown. That's why my father just traveled to Charleston. He went to talk to his friends in the state government about what South Carolina is going to do about this problem. We know our cotton crops can't be harvested without slave labor. Unless we want our world turned over, we've got to resist the Black Republicans. But, we think the big question is whether we'll let the Union government dictate to the states what they can and should do. Most of the people in the South don't think they should be able to do that. South Carolina's now part of a separate country. We'll fight for the right to do what we feel is best for our new country. Now, put away that whip. You don't need it on this plantation. We won't stand for it."

Ely shook his head in disbelief but complied with Will's order. James still lay curled up in a fetal position on the ground where he was hoping for protection from the expected next blow. He drew a full, ragged breath, his first for what seemed a long time. His head was spinning again; he could hardly believe what Master Will had said. He had basically agreed with what both Ned and Joseph had been saying in secret. However, it didn't sound as if South Carolina was going along with what Mister Lincoln was going to tell them to do. Master Will was even talking about fighting a war against the Union government! Just wait until he talked with Joseph tonight! But they would have to be more careful. He certainly didn't want more dances with brother whip! His back stung like fire itself. He could hardly imagine a severe whipping like slaves received on other plantations.

After the excitement, the rest of the day's cotton picking seemed to drag on forever. James's back began hurting him as the salty sweat found its way into the open wound. Nathan looked out of the corner of his eye several times toward James. Should he say, "I told you so," or should he offer sympathy to his younger brother? He knew that back was painful. Stephen was his typical, withdrawn self, except Nathan noticed he was looking around more than usual. His eyes were wide open, and he seemed to be waiting for the next excitement. Hopefully, it wouldn't be another attack. When the slaves heard the wagon wheel ring signifying the end of the work day, they released their breath slowly in a collective sigh as they began their walk back to the cabins.

Hardly a word was exchanged between the brothers on the slow trek until they were almost home. When they arrived at the spring to wash up, Nathan finally broke the long silence.

"Whut you gwine tell Momma bout today, James?"

"Ain't gonna tell her nuttin. She'd jest yell at me and tell me my big mouf got me into trouble." He paused, trying to decide whether to continue. "Nathan, did you hear what Massuh Will dun tell dat white trash? I telled you dat de new president wuz gwine make us be slaves no mo! Ned an Joseph warnt lyin!"

"I heared him," responded Nathan. "I also heared him say dat dis here country wuz gwine be at war iffin dat president tried tuh do dat! He said he hisself was gwine fight for de Souf. My mind kin hardly understand what dat would be lik!"

"Well, don't matter. He can't fight de whole Union jes tuh keep a few ragged niggers. We ain't worth dat! Cotton ain't eben worth dat!"

Nathan helped James take off his shirt. He carefully washed the whip wound with the cool spring water, hoping the gash on his brother's back wouldn't fester up. He told James that he was definitely going to have a scar where the whip struck him.

The boys continued on to the cabin and to Momma. To her complete amazement, the meal passed with no unpleasantness at all. Instead, a thoughtful silence hung so deep you could have cut it with a knife. The boys actually talked about progress made that day in the picking. They allowed as how they might be finished a bit ahead of schedule. They might even get a day or two off before the next chores began, depending on the mood of the overseer on the day they finished.

More of the same thoughtful silence permeated the slave quarters and workplace over the next few weeks. The slaves noticed when the white folks were together, they met in small groups and held discussions which many times turned into quiet arguments. They never said much of anything which could be overheard by the slaves. Even so, the picture of a likely war became painfully clear to them, as bits and pieces and scraps of information were passed from house slaves to field hands to horse tenders to blacksmiths to every other type of laborer on the plantation.

Master Will was heard by one of the house servants in an argument with his father on the front porch of the Big House. His words quickly echoed throughout the plantation: "No, Father—you have too much to do here keeping this plantation going. Mother depends on you, so do the slaves. You can't go fighting a war, much as you would like to! I'm old enough to go defend South Carolina. With my three years at the Citadel, you know I can get a commission as an officer as soon as things break out.

Samuel told me about that cannon-fire at the Yankee ship down in Charleston Harbor, last week. I understand those Yankees fairly flew across the water getting away; just like they will fly away from us as soon as the first shot of war is fired. Those white-faced, soft city-dwellers don't even have a chance against the South. Why, every man in the Low Country has been on horseback and fired guns practically since they were born. So, I'll be safe; it will most likely even be fun! I'll write you and Mother often to let you know what's going on."

Master Richard didn't say much in response, other than having to reluctantly agree with much of what young Will had passionately argued.

"I guess if it all comes to a head and you have to go, we'll outfit you ready for war as well as can be done. I believe we can do a good job of that, but let's worry about it when it happens."

More conversation and more juicy information may have passed between father and son, but this was all the girl could remember and pass on to the other eager listeners back in the slave-quarter clearing that evening.

CHAPTER TWO
THE SOUNDS OF WAR
The Brothers
Spring-Summer, 1861

Even though things were quiet on the surface for the time being, tidbits from the whispered conversations of the white folks were continually passed among the slaves in the evening after dinner. Somehow, information always passed rapidly from those slaves in the Big House down to those in the slave quarters and the fields. The slave conversations were whispered in much smaller groups hidden from the whites.

One night shortly after the house girl had reported on the conversation between Young Master Will and Old Master Richard, Nathan, James, and Stephen were sitting together on some old logs adjacent to the clearing near the slave cabins. They had finished helping Momma with the dishes from dinner.

It was the first time in weeks that Nathan had not seen James huddled with Joseph, and he teased James. "What's de matter little brudder? Joseph run away an hide from you? Stephen and me am real pleasured to hab you sittin wid us sted ob him."

James directed a sharp look at his brother; he didn't respond right away. Finally he sighed and said, "I promise I wouldn't say whar he be, so I can't say."

No amount of poking and prodding by Nathan could make James say anything. Nathan began getting a hollow feeling in the pit of his stomach, sort of like what he got when he hadn't eaten all day. The brothers headed back toward the cabin as the deepening dusk was casting long, almost scary shadows through the palmetto trees. Nathan worried, James was grim, and Stephen seemed puzzled by the whole conversation. The silence continued to lay heavy on all of them through supper. Darkness came and the family fell into a restless sleep.

Early the next morning, even before Momma rousted her brood, a loud commotion woke all the slaves. There were four or five mounted white men in the clearing, all carrying torches. Each saddle horn held a coiled rope, and several carried whips. The yellow, flickering light of the torches added an almost satanic cast to their already ferocious faces.

One of them yelled, "Have any of you seen that worthless niggah, Joseph? He was sent to the next plantation early yesterday evening to fetch something for Master Richard, and we've not seen him since."

There was no answer at all from the assembled sleepy-eyed and terrified slaves, and they began passing each other worried looks.

"Come on, someone must have heard somethin! Talk, or you'll all be sorry." Silence again was the only answer the white men received.

"Where's that boy James," one of the whites asked. "He's been seen with Joseph lots of evenings. Maybe they were plottin up this runaway for Joseph!"

Nathan shielded James with his body, hoping against hope the men would not spot him in the dark shadows around the clearing.

But his effort was to no avail, as one of the white men saw him and yelled, "Come here boy. Tell us what you know, or it will go very bad for you. I can promise you that!"

"I don't know nothin, Massuh," pleaded James. "Honest, I didn see Joseph all day yesterday. I didn eben see him here las night."

"Boy, if I find out you're lyin to me about this," exclaimed Ely, "The little whippin I gave you the other day won't seem like nothin. I'll whup you till you can't stand up; then I'll whup on you some more!"

Nathan heard Momma sharply inhale and give a quiet gasp. He turned in a hurry to see if she was all right; her face looked as if she had been whipped herself. After more bullying and threatening, the men rode away, loudly promising that if they caught Joseph and brought him back, he would definitely wish he had never been born. Then they'd find out who of the other slaves helped him and they'd be just as sorry.

Nathan stole another sideways look at Momma's face. The almost-whipped look he had seen earlier had been replaced by another look that Nathan knew all too well--the dark and brooding thundercloud, filled with thunder and lightning.

"Uh-oh," thought Nathan, "There'll be the debil to pay now!" The brothers went back into the cabin with their mother, dreading what was to come.

Momma softly said, "Which one ob you'uns wants tuh tell me bout dis whuppin?"

Nathan, James, and Stephen looked at each other, but no one said anything.

James shrugged his shoulders, then said, "Aw Momma, it wuz

jest dat trash overseer! Dat buckra ask me somethin and when he didn't like whut I telled him, he jest whupped me one time. I didn't figger it wuz eny big ting, so I didn tell you. Don't be mad at Nathan or Stephen. Dey didn tell you cause I ast dem not tuh."

Momma responded, "I ain't mad at no one. Ize jest hurt cause ya'll kept secrets from your own Momma. If'in we're gwine tuh get thru dis war thing alive, we haz tuh stick together. No more secrets from yore Momma!"

The boys hurried and gladly agreed, and James blurted out, "Momma, I wuz tellin' de truf when I told dose men dat I didn know whar Joseph wuz. I ain't seed him!"

Nathan said, "I hope he wuzn't stupid enuff tuh run away. Iffen dey don kill him when dey ketch him, dey'll likely near kill him fore dey git him back."

Things returned to the quiet times of the past several weeks, and the brothers worked hard along with the rest of the field hands in completing the early cotton harvest. The weather even cooperated as the high cottony clouds provided some relief from the scalding sun. The whispered conversations among the whites continued, swiftly being echoed among the slaves. It seemed to grow in intensity as more news and rumors of the coming war arrived daily.

About two weeks after the early morning confrontation with the runaway-hunting whites, Nathan got an unusual message from one of the household servants that Master Will wanted to talk with him about what the field hands were to do next, since the cotton harvest was practically over. Nathan felt quite proud that he was chosen to go to the Big House, and after cleaning up, he ran the entire way to the house.

As Nathan approached the white mansion with the tall columns, he felt somewhat overwhelmed by the sheer size of the Big House. On this visit, he was to get no further than the front porch, itself quite a sumptuous place for Nathan. The porch was probably one hundred feet long, all whitewashed, and the rail, about waist-high, was the fanciest woodworking that Nathan had ever seen. The posts supporting the porch rail were carved in a spiral pattern. The furniture on the porch was as fancy as any Nathan had seen, with several conversation centers of chairs, chaise lounges, and small tables for drinks and the cigars which the gentlemen enjoyed daily after dinner.

Nathan had just arrived on the long porch of the Big House when two scruffy-looking white men rode up, trailing dust and a horse with a bundle of dirty rags tied across the saddle. When Master Richard and his family came out, one of the men cut the rope holding the bundle on the horse. As it tumbled to the ground, they realized that the bundle was a man.

Master Will ran out to the downed man and examined him closely. "It's Joseph! They've almost killed him!"

One of the men explained, "We ketched him over to Memphis with several other runaways trying tuh sneak on a riverboat headin North. He was real stubborn about who he belonged tuh, so we had tuh loosen up his tongue a bit before he told us that he belonged to this place. He needs a little healin, but since he's alive we claim the runaway slave reward. We'll jest take our fifty dollars and be on our way. We have several other stops tuh make, and we ain't got time tuh argue."

Master Richard rose and went back into the house. He returned with his pocketbook and counted off fifty dollars for the man. His body language and facial expression showed his utter contempt for the man and his companions.

"I don't approve of what you did to this slave. There isn't a square inch of him that isn't beat or bloodied, but the law is the law. Here's your blood money. Now get off my land and don't ever let me see you here again!"

The man flashed an evil grin, stowed the bills in a dirty shirt pocket, and tipped his hat. He retorted, "Pleasure doin business with you. Don't plan tuh come back this way nohow. If you kept your slaves under control, there'd be no work for the likes ob us."

"I give you thirty seconds to be gone, or I'm turning the hunting dogs loose on you," said Master Richard. The men wheeled their horses around and rode off into the dusk.

Master Will and Nathan carefully carried Joseph around back to the kitchen. Between the two of them with help from several of the household servants, they cleaned Joseph and bound most of his wounds. They then waited for the doctor to arrive.

Finally he got there and looked Joseph over to determine whether there were any internal wounds. "He's in pretty bad shape, but I reckon he'll survive. However, I wouldn't count on getting any work out of him for a bit."

Will asked Nathan to stay with Joseph and watch over him until he revived. Nathan lowered himself to the hard wooden floor and went to sleep next to Joseph's pallet.

At 3:00 o'clock in the morning, Nathan was awakened from a sound sleep by a moan.

"Whar am I?" asked Joseph. "It hurts turrble bad."

Nathan replied, "You am back on de plantation. Dem trash bounty hunters bout half killed you, but de doctor said you'd likely live. Now hesh and gwine to sleep."

Joseph fell back into a restless sleep. His moans and groans kept Nathan awake the remainder of the night. Master Will came around to the kitchen the next morning to check on Joseph. Finding him awake and alert, he sent Nathan back down to the slave quarters to begin the day's work.

Before he left, Master Will told Nathan, "We'll talk another time about the work to come."

Nathan left, feeling a little let down by the loss of his big moment to talk and plan with the master. Field hands seldom saw any of the Big House folks except for special occasions and maybe on Sunday mornings when they attended services at the small Episcopal chapel.

When he got back to the palmetto clearing of the slave quarters, Nathan was immediately surrounded by the other slaves. They hurled dozens of questions at him, sounding all at the same time. He relished being the center of attention as he told the story of what had happened. He explained the events in great detail, especially how badly hurt Joseph was. After most of the other slaves had left for the fields and Big House for their day's work, Nathan turned on James.

"Now, little brudder, I weren't goin tuh say I telled you so, but I haz tuh! See what happens when you doesn't behave and do as youse am told? What iffen dat had been you! An tink ob how Momma and us would hab felt iffen dat had been you dem men cut off'n dat hoss!"

To Nathan's surprise, James looked down at the ground and idly drew a circle in the dust with his bare right big toe. "I hates dat it happened tuh Joseph. I telled him dat he couldn't git away tuh de North now. Maybe iffen he wait till de war starts, but not now!"

Nathan realized there was no use of further talking. He didn't chastise James for having known that Joseph was intent on escaping and not telling his family. Instead, he turned away and started walking in the direction of the cotton field where the remnants of cotton waited to be collected. He had to admit that he was a little proud of his brother for keeping his secret in the face of threats from the slavers. Without a word, James picked up his canvas shoulder bag and followed him.

The savagely hot day crept by. Even the temporary relief that the high cumulus clouds had given was gone. The sun beat down through the clear Carolina sky with a vengeance. The slaves were ordered to go back over the once-picked plants to salvage what few small pods remained scattered across the field. It was a much less rewarding task now, as the bags filled more slowly.

The overseer constantly taunted all of the field hands about

Joseph and his condition, but he saved his worst for James. James did not respond with either words or looks as the overseer's verbal attack increased in intensity as the day wore on; he just kept on picking cotton. Nathan was proud of him.

To everyone's relief, the old wagon wheel's melodious tone finally sounded from the Big House. The slaves tossed their partially-filled bags into the wagon and trudged back toward the clearing in silence.

Dinner at the boys' cabin was passed in the same silence. James ate very little supper as he pushed the food from one side of his plate to another with his cornbread. Momma related the bits of news she had heard from one of the house slaves. Joseph was expected to recover, but he would have some terrible scars that would be with him the rest of his life. His back was criss-crossed with whip tracks that stood out in angry scars.

James looked up for the first time during the meal and commented, "I bet he's also got eben bigger scars down inside him dat you can't see; doze he will hav for jes as long or eben longer."

CHAPTER THREE
THE BEGINNING
Nathan
Spring, 1861

Life plodded along at the plantation through March as the South Carolina winter ended and spring began. The only notable event was the inauguration of midwesterner Abraham Lincoln as president of the United States. He faced the eminent secession of the Southern states. He had stated that he had no intention of interfering with slavery in those states where it already existed, but would oppose its establishment in those territories which wished to join the Union. The reaction of the whites on the plantation was predictable--they did not believe him. Preparation and discussion continued for the war that they believed to be inevitable. The slaves also had predictable reactions to the rumors they heard about Lincoln's early statements.

They wanted to believe Lincoln but mumbled and grumbled amongst themselves. "He is de same as all de rest. Ain't nothin or nobody goin eber tuh set us free! We're bound tuh dis life for de rest ob ours an probbly our chilluns as well."

The pace at the plantation quickened as the slaves began preparation to plant another crop of cotton. The cycle appeared both inevitable and endless in the Low Country with its almost continuous growing seasons. At least in the areas of the country where winter was experienced, you get a short rest between growing seasons; here, you plant virtually as soon as you complete the prior crop.

In April, all hell broke loose when word came that the South Carolina militia had fired on the United States fort, Sumter in Charleston. The news swiftly spread among all of the inhabitants of the plantation, black and white, Big House and slave quarters alike. The patriotic war fever spread among the people in the Big House, and Master Richard began preparations to send his son off to war in grand style.

Tailors were brought in and measurements made; slaves were tasked to make the finest set of horse trappings ever seen in the Low Country; horses were checked carefully for looks, speed, and endurance. Young Master Will contacted the Citadel which referred him to Commandant Stevens. Stevens was in the process of setting up a legion for defense of the State of South Carolina, particularly on the Atlantic Ocean coastline, thought to be the most likely area where the Yankees would first come. Master Will took the three-day horse trip to Charleston, where Colonel Stevens was located, and returned some two weeks later.

He arrived home in a state of excitement that was described by one of the house slaves, as "I figgered dat he wuz bound tuh splode eny time, he wuz so cited. Old Massuh Richard wuz so proud hiz buttons wuz bout tuh pop!"

Master Will had returned bearing a commission as Second Lieutenant in the newly-formed Holcombe Legion. He was instructed to return to Charleston within the month to begin service. As the time for his departure neared, the preparations for outfitting the young warrior intensified even from their early fast pace, as people scrambled in all directions at once.

Only the house slaves were involved with the preparations, so the dreary life in the cotton fields didn't change much for Nathan, James, and Stephen as the planting continued. The worthy news items kept on moving from Big House to slave quarters as fast as a man riding a racehorse could have delivered messages.

A much quieter, subdued Joseph returned to work in the fields. Persistent questioning from James and the other field hands brought no response at all about what had happened to him during his brief flight. Nathan also noticed that Joseph refused to remove his shirt even when the temperature became intolerable in the fields on sunny days.

"Don't wants tuh talk nuttin bout it," was his only answer.

Eventually the questions ceased, and Joseph was gradually accepted back into the fold. The other field hands were quite careful about being seen talking with the ex-runaway, for fear of getting that extra attention that they were all anxious to avoid. The best way to survive was never to be noticed by the white overseers.

One day in the midst of the planting, a most singular thing happened. As Nathan and the other field hands were slowly placing the cotton seeds in rows and covering them with the rich black topsoil, one of the house slaves came running across the field looking for the overseer. Finding him, he spoke quietly to the man, who looked in Nathan's direction.

"Come here, Niggah," he yelled to Nathan. "I don't know what you've done, but your black ass is deep in trouble now. Git back tuh your cabin and clean up. They want you up at the Big House, right now! Git movin—yore feet took root?"

Nathan swallowed his heart; his tongue stuck to the roof of his mouth. As he followed the house slave hurrying across the field and back to the slave cabin clearing, he felt worse and worse. As he passed the field where Momma was working with the other women field hands, she looked up and saw Nathan with the house slave. She stood up, and as her mouth opened, she put her hands over her heart as if she felt a severe pain.

Nathan's mind raced through possibilities and impossibilities. He thought back over the past few weeks, trying to remember anytime when he might have caused one of the white folks some problem. He couldn't think of anything he might have done. Maybe they aim to sell me, is all he could think of.

He talked out loud to himself, "I sho hate's dat--I don't want tuh leave Momma and my brudders, but I don reckon I hab any choice. I kin see mebbe why James feels like he does bout bein a slave. It's turbble not havin no say in whut people do tuh you!"

The two arrived breathless at Nathan's cabin.

"Git cleaned up boy, quick! Put on yore Sunday clothes," panted the house slave. "I doesn't know whut dey wants wid you, but dey say for me tuh git you up dar quick, and I aims tuh do jest dat an stay out ob trubble myself!"

Nathan hurriedly wiped off the accumulated sweat of the day and washed himself down at the spring. He threw on his Sunday-go-to-meeting clothes and presented himself for the inspection of the house slave, who said, "I reckon dat you looks all rite."

The two slaves began the journey up toward the Big House. Nathan continued speculation about the evil that was about to befall him. He felt worse and worse with every step he took. His feet were heavier with each step, but they continued moving with no urging from him, as if he were on a treadmill.

After the almost endless trip, they arrived at the long magnolia-lined drive that led to the Big House, where both the Masters waited on the expansive front porch. Nathan looked around; even anticipation of whatever was to come couldn't totally overwhelm the splendor of the porch. But the trepidation that Nathan felt in facing the unknown wouldn't allow him the thrill he usually felt in the first glimpse of the Big House.

"Where were you, boy, Charleston?" asked Old Master Richard. Nathan's leaden heart seemed to sink even further, if that was possible. He shuffled his feet on the smooth wood of the step.

To Nathan's surprise, Master Will smiled at his father and said, "Don't scare him to death with your growls, Father! I said that I'd take care of this matter--you promised me the servant I wanted, remember?"

"All right, I guess I do seem to recollect saying that," responded Old Master Richard. His scowl disappeared, replaced with a slight smile. "Go ahead."

Nathan's puzzlement grew even beyond the possible stretches of his already overworked imagination. He held his breath and felt and heard his own heartbeat in his chest. He listened to Master Will, dreading the yet unspoken words.

"Nathan," began Master Will, "I will serve the Confederacy as an officer in the Holcombe Legion. In this position I'm allowed and will need a personal body servant. My father has kindly permitted me to select whomever I want from this plantation. I've thought about it since I returned from Charleston, and I've watched all of the servants work. I've decided that you're the servant that I want to go with me."

Nathan thought he would faint dead away. His head whirled and spun, and his knees turned to water. He felt incapable of speech. This was certainly not one of the many possibilities he had thought of at all! The dreaded word "sold" hadn't surfaced. The anticipation of the worst was replaced with euphoria. His capability to speak still escaped him.

"Don't you have anything at all to say? What do you think?"

"But, Massuh," stammered Nathan. He thought to himself that he sounded like a croaking pond frog during spring mating season. "Thar am so many slaves older and smarter than I iz--I ain't nebber eben been a house slave! Iz yo sho dat I is de one yo wants?"

"Nathan," Master Will answered softly. "I told you that I had been observing all of the slaves over the past week. I've seen that you work hard and steady. You cause no trouble. You're always in a good mood. That's just what I'm looking for, someone who will be there when I need assistance; someone who doesn't seem to let every little thing bother him. As we go to war, you'll soon find that it's a difficult task that I'm giving you. It will be difficult, dirty, and likely dangerous. But the laws of South Carolina give their officers the right to keep one body servant with them and will even pay for a horse for you. Now, what do you think?"

Nathan's head reeled as consequences, responsibilities, and possibilities whirled through his mind like sun sparkles on the pond. "Massuh, I reckons dat iffen Ize de one you wants, den Ize de one you gits. I'll work hard an try tuh be no bother tuh you."

"That's all I can ask for. Now, we leave day after tomorrow, so start getting your things together. I reckon we'll have to put the tailors to work making you a set of clothes. It certainly won't do having the personal body servant of a Second Lieutenant in the Holcombe Legion looking like a field hand."

Nathan stood frozen for a minute. "Git!" Master Will jokingly shouted. "If you stay rooted to that spot much longer, I may come to believe that I've made a mistake. Then I'd have to look elsewhere for my body servant; someone who isn't so lazy and slow!"

"Ize going, Massuh Will," said Nathan. "Ize gitting as fast as these legs kin carry me. You ain't makin no mistake, I promise you dat!"

Nathan shouted these last words over his shoulder as he sprinted in the direction of the slave quarters. As he left he could still hear the laughter of both the young and old masters at his parting words.

He heard Old Master Richard say, "I wondered at first if you'd made a mistake in not choosing one of our older, more mature slaves; now I believe that you've chosen very wisely."

Nathan practically flew through the palmetto and pine woods toward the slave cabins. He headed straight for his cabin and burst through the door, looking for someone, anyone, to tell his exciting news. Momma had returned from the fields early and was standing by the stove and brought him up straight.

"Boy! Don't you never come into dis house like dat no moe! You bout scairt me tuh death. Now, calm yourself down and gwine back outside an come back in here. Only dis time, do it right! My poor old heart can't stand no moe ob dis."

But as Nathan went outside and re-entered the cabin with less speed this time, Momma's questions did not slow up at all—if anything, they intensified.

"Whut's got into you? Why ain't you back out in de cotton fields? What dey wants wid you up at de Big House? What have you dun? Is you in trubble?"

Nathan took a deep breath to calm himself down. He wanted to tell Momma the news in as grownup a fashion as he felt at that time. As soon as Momma stopped talking to take a breath, he jumped in.

"Momma, Momma, gives me a chanct to answer you questions. Massuh Will dun chose me tuh be his body servant tuh gwine off tuh de war wit him. He's gittin me a hoss, clothes, and everthin! He choosed me ober all de slaves on de plantation!"

To Nathan's great surprise, Momma just stood there in silence. Then he saw several alligator tears emerge from her eyes and track through the dust on her cheeks. She once again placed both of her hands on her heart.

"What's de mattuh, Momma?" asked Nathan, worried now as he moved to stand by her side. He placed his arm around her quivering shoulders.

"My baby's goin off tuh war and probbly gwine git hisself kilt, dat's what's de mattuh," Momma now sobbed as if her ample heart was splitting in two.

"No, Momma. Ize not gwine tuh be a sojer, jest a body servant! Dey would never gibs no slave a gun." Nathan looked his Momma in the eyes. "I won't be in de war whar I kin git myself kilt! You knows dat no Yankee kin hurts Massuh Will or me. Cides, Massuh kin whale a dozen ob em fore coffee is hot, in a fair fight!"

Momma returned his look of confidence with her own look of suspicion. She was a long way from being convinced.

"Whut do a body servant do in de war?" she asked him. The mother and son sat at the rickety old table that served the family at meal times.

Nathan tried to explain what Will had told him about him working hard and not causing trouble and being cheerful, but it made little sense as the words tumbled out.

"Massuh Will telled me dat I wuz tuh hep him, ride my hoss, an, an, an, I don't rightly know whut else Ize supposed tuh do! I reckon meybe I kin ask when I goes tuh de Big House tuh hab dat tailor make me some clothes. Massuh Will said it wouldn't do tuh haz me looks like a field hand, iffn I wuz tuh be his body servant. Ize posed tuh gwine back up dar to de Big House tomorrow mornin, firs ting. I ain't posed to go to de fields, jes de Big House."

Nathan and Momma both fell silent as their minds played with the question Momma had asked. They were just like most folks—even bad situations were tolerable if they were familiar. It was when changes or unfamiliar situations appeared that worry cropped up.

When his brothers returned weary and sweaty from the cotton fields that evening, Nathan went through the story again from start to finish.

Stephen was excited for Nathan and asked with a twinkle in his eye, "Do dat mean you won't has tuh pick cotton no moe wid us pore ole field slaves?"

Nathan laughed. "At least not as long as de war last; maybe after. Massuh Will said dat dey don't guess dat de war will last long, dat's fer sartin. Dey spect dat dem Yankees will cut and run as soon as de shootin start. De white folk at de Big House spect de war will be ober in tree, four month, tops. Dat's what dey figger."

James had remained ominously quiet during the whole discussion. Suddenly he burst out, "I reckon dat dis mean dat you'uns will be helpin fight fer us tuh stay slaves. Dat's da way I figgers it. I don't lik it, don't lik it a'tall!"

Momma exploded. "James, you hush yore big mouth! Nathan has a chance tuh be somthin oder than a field hand, and Ize happy fer him! You hush dat Joseph slave talk and you be happy fer yore big bruder!"

As usual, James wasn't able to hold forth against Momma, so he bit his tongue and remained silent for the rest of the evening. Even at his young age, he had developed a thundercloud look that came close to Momma's, and he now utilized that look to express his dissatisfaction with the situation.

Early the next morning, as the dusky light of dawn broke over the slave cabins, a different house slave appeared at the clearing as Nathan finished his breakfast and James and Stephen were preparing to go into the cotton fields with the other field hands.

"Nathan, dey told me to come down here and git you. Dey wants you up at the Big House--dat tailor is comin and dey needs tuh measure you."

Momma said, "Nathan, I don't reckon I knows what we will do wid you! Two days, two trips tuh de Big House an new clothes. I spose you am gittin tuh be some big man, dat's whut!"

Nathan drew himself up to his full height and replied, "Momma, I ain't no big man. Ize jest a body servant, but I plans tuh be de best body servant Ize kin be. I'm gwine show Massuh Will dat he didn't make no mistake when he choosed me. I needs to talk to you bout how you makes cornbred—I spec I needs to larn dat."

After this dignified declaration about his intentions, Nathan followed the house slave up to the Big House. He was escorted into the huge front hall, then into Master Richard's study. The interior of that room fit Nathan's idea of what a palace would look like. The walls of the room were paneled with a dark, rich wood which gleamed like sunlight, the result of the house servants' many hours of hard work, waxing and polishing. The furniture in the room consisted of big overstuffed chairs and sofas, covered with leather, and the gleaming wood floor was partially covered with expensive oriental rugs.

The tailor fitted Nathan for what looked to him like Sunday clothes. The man measured Nathan every direction imaginable, and Nathan was relieved when the session was over and all the measurements recorded. Master Will told the man to make two sets of clothes so his body servant would always be sharp. Nathan's poor head almost exploded with that statement—one new set of clothes was overwhelming—two was incomprehensible.

That afternoon, Nathan returned to his cabin carrying a paper-wrapped package under his arm and with great pride showed his new outfits to Momma, James, and Stephen when they returned from the field that evening. James remained quiet, while Stephen was more excited for his big brother and wanted to talk more than usual. Nathan became progressively quieter and preoccupied. Momma finally noticed and asked him what was the matter. Nathan looked at her with a different emotion--he had fear in his eyes.

"We'uns leave tomorrow, and I ain't nebber bin away from ya'll, cept fer dat one night when I went wid Massuh Will tuh dat oder plantation. I ain't nebber bin out ob dis here county. Ize gwine miss you'uns someting turbble! Plus, I still don't know whut Ize posed to do when I acts lik a body servant!"

Momma clucked like the old hen that guarded her chicks around the edge of the clearing, "Chile, chile, you'll do jest fine! You'uns gwine be de best body servant dem sojers ebber seen! Don't worry—Massuh Will's gwine tell you whut you needs to do and when to do it. Now, it's time tuh go tuh bed, else you'll fall asleep tomorrow an tumble offen dat hoss on your way tuh Charleston. Then Massuh Will knows fer sho dat he dun made a big mistake, an you will be back in de cotton fields wid us, a'pickin dat cotton fer de rest of you natral born life."

The night outside the cabin was still and dark, passing in peace and quiet. Inside, Nathan tossed and turned. The few times he dropped off into a fitful sleep, his mind played games with him, and he dreamed. Most dreams took him back to his childhood. The happy times he could remember were mostly when he was a small child, before he was initiated into the field hand ranks.

Nathan remembered back to when he was only five years old, and he dreamed of one Sunday morning. When the family awoke, Momma fixed a good breakfast. Then, even before the dishes were washed, she tossed the three small boys into the large cast iron kettle out front, where she also made lye soap. She scrubbed the three of them until Nathan complained that he had no skin left. Momma scoffed, then carefully dressed them in their best church clothes. She sat them down on the front porch, and threatened them with a whipping if they moved, much less got dirty.

They sat completely still on the porch for a few minutes, when the strangest thing happened. A small gray field mouse poked his nose out of a hole in the side of the house on the porch. Nathan swore that the mouse looked directly at him, then winked an eye. The small rodent scurried across the porch, jumped to the ground, then ran across the yard. Without saying a word to each other, the three boys picked themselves up and headed out after the mouse, as if the three were occupying one body. They chased the small troublemaker in circles, each one of them coming close to catching him several times.

Everything was fine until Momma walked out on the porch, spotted the boys, and let out a shriek that James said later was an awful lot like hog calling. They screeched to a stop; that is, almost a stop. Baby Stephen fell headlong into a mudhole; then, he was followed closely by James and Nathan. Their free fall was much like dominoes falling in a row. Momma let out one more shriek; then as the boys climbed to their feet, she did a most unusual thing. She covered her mouth with both hands for just a moment. Then, Nathan swore he could see her shoulders shaking. Was she crying? Nathan couldn't tell.

Then, a muffled sound came from behind her hands. It grew in intensity, louder and louder. It was a laugh. It became a belly laugh, and Poppa, who had been watching Momma in anticipation of the explosion to come, joined in. As the boys looked sheepishly at each other, they could see what was so funny. They were literally covered with mud from head to toe. There was absolutely nothing about any of them that was clean. Their eyes gleamed out of their mud caked faces. Momma finally quit laughing, then shrugged her shoulders. She put them back into the kettle, clothes and all, and washed them again.

By this time it was too late to go to church, so all five of them put on their everyday clothes and walked down to the pond, where they ate a picnic lunch and spent the day simply lying around. Nathan and his father fished, and the two younger boys played with Momma. Nathan shook his head, as he struggled awake. He hadn't thought about that afternoon for a long time! He smiled as he relived that day, then forced himself to lie back down.

Nathan still could not go back to sleep; the anticipation of the great event on the morrow overcame him, and more possibilities and issues came to his mind. Each time he thought he had resolved an issue and was about to fall asleep, a new one jumped in uninvited, to cause him to start the whole process again. When dawn came at long last, he was sure he hadn't slept a wink.

Nathan ate the special breakfast Momma had fixed with corn cakes, bacon and fresh milk, then showed real speed as he dressed in his fine new clothes. Momma looked proud as a peacock, and Stephen laughed in delight and clapped his hands. Even James allowed as how brother Nathan looked mighty fine. At long last, James and Stephen both hugged Nathan, shouldered their hoes, and in no great hurry, they walked toward the fields that held their day's work. Momma stood there in proud silence with her arms wrapped in a tight grip around her bosom.

Nathan hurried to say, "No more cryin Momma. I'll be fine. I'll try tuh git word back tuh you when I kin, and I spect you will hear now and den from de house folks dat Massuh Will and me am well."

He gave Momma a big hug and extricated himself before she could soak his new clothes by more crying. Nathan set off on what was to be the greatest adventure of his young life.

☐ ☐ ☐ ☐

CHAPTER FOUR
OFF TO WAR : THEN THERE WERE TWO
Nathan
Summer, 1861

On the 15th of July, as he arrived up at the Big House, Nathan was sure that there had never been so much activity anywhere on the plantation. Master Will was all dressed up in his officer uniform, complete with shiny sword and pistol hanging from his side. All the house servants were lined up to see the young master off to war. Several of them couldn't hide their pride in how fine Nathan looked, as he prepared to accompany his master on the journey.

Will, after hugging his parents and sisters, put his foot in the stirrup and settled with style and grace into his saddle. He turned to Nathan and said, "Let's go. We don't want to be late and miss seeing those Yankees cut and run. There's your horse over there. I need you to lead the pack horse beyond him."

Nathan tried stammering out something to Master Will who showed little patience as he cut him off. "I said let's go, Nathan!"

Nathan struggled to get his foot into the stirrup and pulled hard on the saddle horn. He finally succeeded in stepping up only to fall right off the other side of the saddle. Nathan, in his new clothes, collapsed into a pitiful heap in the dust.

After everyone had a good laugh, Nathan said, "Please, Massuh Will, dat's whut I wuz tryin tuh tell you. I ain't nebber rid no hoss. Jest old slab-sided mules, whar onct you git on, you can't falls off cause he be so wide!"

Will laughed more gently, "Get back on him, Nathan. This time hold on tight to that horn on the saddle. The horse will do what you want him to do. Let him know who's the boss, that's all."

"Rite now, he be de boss, dat's fer shore!" stammered Nathan. This time Nathan laughed with everyone.

Nathan did as he was told and eventually found himself seated on his horse. The two set off for war, a finely-dressed, gracefully-outfitted young officer and a dusty slave, holding on the saddle horn with all of his strength and bouncing high with every step the horse took. They looked for all the world like Cervantes's Don Quixote and his sidekick Sancho riding off to tilt at windmills. However, Will and the rest of the rapidly expanding Confederate Army whom they would join in Columbia hoped that their quest would find a more definitive ending with the rout of the Yankees and with no windmills!

Will and Nathan rode hard all day, taking only a couple of brief rest and relief stops. Nathan had a difficult time enjoying the scenery of the Low Country because of the ever-increasing pains in his legs and back. As the South Carolina dusk finally approached and the long shadows of evening appeared, Will turned around in his saddle to look at Nathan.

"Well, I guess we'd better stop for the night. Time for you to find out what being a body servant is all about!" Will slid with as much style and grace as he had exhibited that morning from his horse and tethered him to a nearby low-hanging branch. "Now, Nathan, we'll start with . . . Nathan! What are you still doing up on that horse?"

"Massuh Will, Ize powerful sorry and Ize tried several times, but I can't git off'n dis hoss! My legs don't work no mo'!"

Master Will chuckled. "Riding can really get to you when you're not used to it. I guess that we've made a long day of it. We've sure covered a lot of ground. It's been a very successful first day of travel. Here, let me help you get off that horse."

Will pushed on Nathan's right side, and Nathan, no more gracefully than he had first mounted the horse that morning, promptly slid off the horse onto the hard ground. As he lay in a heap in the dust, he moaned not so softly. He tried without success several more times to stand up, but returned clumsily to Mother Earth each time.

He cried out, "Massuh Will, my legs still don't work! Dey can't ebben carry me at all! What is I tuh do, effen Ize can't nebber walk again? I can't be no body serbent, den."

Will broke out in loud laughter, then explained more softly, "Your legs not work very well now, but they'll be better in the morning. Here, let me help you to that log over there, and maybe you'll be all right in a little while."

He deposited Nathan on a moss-covered log under the low hanging branches of the big shade tree where they had stopped for the night. Will worked with speed and efficiency to set up the two small tents they had brought with them, collect fire wood, and start a small campfire. He set a fire-blackened coffee pot on the fire and cooked a simple dinner. He brought a plate over to Nathan.

After Nathan and Will ate dinner and each had a cup of coffee, Will leaned back and lit his pipe and gave a contented sigh. Nathan, in spite of the pain in his stiff limbs, managed to enjoy the meal, as well as the coffee with plenty of sugar, the first time he had ever tried that delicacy. Although he didn't say so, the irony of the situation was not lost on Nathan; he enjoyed the role reversal where Will was waiting on him hand and foot.

Nathan sat there for just a minute, then timidly asked, "Massuh Will, I bin meanin tuh ask and nobuddy seem tuh know--what xactly do a body servant do when he gwine off tuh war?"

Will exploded in laughter, almost choking on his pipe. When he regained his breath, he said, "Nathan, have you been watching what I've been doing for the past several hours? Set up the tents, started a fire, cooked dinner, and waited on you? That's what a body servant does! Tonight, I've been your body servant! All you have to do to make me happy is do as well as I've done at being a body servant, and keep my uniform looking sharp.

You will have other other duties; keep our quarters clean, wash clothes, shine boots, polish swords and buckles, run errands, and go to the commissary to get the rations you need to cook our meals. If you do all those tasks well throughout the war, when it's over, I'll talk with my father about giving you your freedom. If he agrees, that's what we'll do."

After this startling pronouncement, Will retired to his tent for the night, leaving a befuddled and confused Nathan, who once again found sleeping very difficult. His mind wandered between trying to understand exactly what Will had said and trying to comprehend the concept of freedom. He was embarrassed about Will waiting on him instead of the other way around, and managed to continually find parts of his body so sore that he couldn't get comfortable. Finally, in the wee hours of the morning, exhaustion took over, and Nathan fell into a deep, dreamless sleep.

When he awoke in the early hours of a new morning, Nathan found himself stiff, but at least he was again able to walk, although with much pain and no speed. He kicked the almost dead coals from last night's fire, added new wood, and soon had the coffee pot bubbling. He didn't move with any coordination, but at least he was able to move around.

He woke Master Will and cheerfully said, "See Massuh Will, I kin be a good body servant! I kin be de bes body servant you has ebber seed!"

Master Will laughed and said, "I would hope so! After all, you had a good teacher! Now, after breakfast we need to get those tents packed and tied on the horses, and we'll get a little further towards Charleston. We're due there in a couple of days, and I want to help with the organizing of the Legion. Get moving!"

Nathan moved as fast as his aching and creaking body permitted. He completed his tasks, and they were soon on their way down the road. Although the first few steps of the horse, particularly as he jumped skittishly with early morning enthusiasm, were pure agony for Nathan, he rode slightly better than he had the day before. He didn't bounce quite as far into the air with every step the horse took. He was able to keep up with Master Will with a little more success, as shown by the fact that Will didn't have to wait for him quite as often. He also released the death grip on the saddle horn; at least some of the time. This day, he enjoyed seeing new sights as they rode through a different portion of the Low Country.

Nathan worked hard for the next two days at his new trade, learning little things which pleased Master Will. He figured that the more Master Will got to sit or lie by the campfire smoking his pipe and the less he had to tell Nathan to do, the better job he was doing at becoming a good body servant.

When they arrived in Charleston late Friday evening, Will instructed Nathan to join the other body servants near the edge of the field full of tents, while he joined the officers for the night in the plantation house that had been commandeered for their headquarters. Nathan did as he was told. He set up his own tent, ate his supper, and then walked over to the body servants at their campfire.

In the discussions around the campfire, Nathan found the other Negroes to be pretty much like the slaves at home. Some grumbled about being in danger during the fighting and all the hard work they were going to have to do. Others, like Nathan, were simply happy to be placed in circumstances different from their dull daily routines. Still others just gave every indication of being in a total state of confusion and were bumfuzzled at their present surroundings. Nathan listened carefully to all that was said and offered no comments of his own.

The evening passed, and quiet, as well as darkness, gradually descended on the camp. Nathan lay in his tent and watched the coals of the campfire through the tent flaps as they grew dimmer and dimmer, finally twinkling away to darkness. In the coals he saw a progressing collection of pictures, mostly of Momma, his brothers, and his home back on the plantation. His collection of mental pictures finally dimmed like the campfire, and he drifted into a dreamless sleep, the best sleep he had enjoyed for weeks, since this whole adventure had first been discussed back on the plantation.

The next morning Nathan was not completely sure what was expected of him, but that was settled when Master Will came over to the servants' quarters and told Nathan to follow him. He showed Nathan where his tent was to be, and Nathan started right away to work on Will's coffee and breakfast. Nathan proved to be a quick learner, and over the weeks to come, he effectively picked up the attributes of a first-rate military scrounger.

Nathan worked hard and fit Master Will's tent with a wooden floor, using scrap boards he found out in the countryside. He provided many additional amenities making his master's life a little more bearable. Many of the body servants in the Legion, as in most Confederate units, became special experts in the foraging business. Several became renown for their expertise in stealing chickens without getting caught. The servants were quite willing to teach their fellows their new-found skills, and Nathan learned many tricks of the trade from more experienced men.

Nathan settled down in a routine, and soon the days stretched into weeks and the weeks into months. Camp continued until the men felt the stirrings of winter. After learning all of his duties and refining them, Nathan found that the life of a body servant was really not a hard one, at least not in this long-term camp. He had ample opportunity to loaf around the camp but had to be careful not to get trapped in some of the activities of the other servants; many became enamored with gambling, including cock fights, cards, and dice. Nathan had only to close his eyes for just a moment, and picture Momma's famous thundercloud expression to make it easy to pass up these distractions.

Nathan discovered that one of his unspoken duties, perhaps one of the most important, was helping with the morale of the camp. His normal good-natured attitude seemed to brighten other's dispositions when he was with the soldiers or officers. He took their natural ribbing and practical jokes well, and he soon became one of the favorites of the servants among the white members of the Legion. He found the fine line of trouble when teasing the whites and was able to get revenge for some of the teasing of him without making anyone mad.

This favorite son position helped Nathan get into another pastime. After listening to some of the other slaves talk about the many soldiers in the Legion who did not have body servants, Nathan realized that this might be a place for an entrepreneurial spirit. He checked his idea out with Will, and his master told him he had no problem with the idea, as long as it didn't interfere with his body servant duties.

So, Nathan went into business, advertising among the foot soldiers that he would wash socks for a paltry five cents per pair. Although throughout the war the soldiers were able to make do with a poor clothing allotment, clean socks were an important factor for decent morale brought on by healthy feet.

Alongside his tent, Nathan set up a large black soap-making kettle and started a fire under it every morning after he finished his regular chores of cooking, cleaning, and polishing. When he got the water boiling, he tossed in the dozen or so pairs of filthy, smelly socks, which seemed to have magically appeared in a pile by his tent during the night. He let the soiled socks boil for a bit. He scrubbed each sock using strong lye soap, then arranged them to dry on a nearby split-rail fence. Somehow, the owners could always recognize their socks, and they would pick them up that evening and pay Nathan. He amassed what he considered to be quite a fortune in Confederate dollars.

Later in the war, Nathan was able to exchange some of this currency for real gold, which he sewed into his jacket lining. His jacket became heavy, but Nathan didn't mind the extra weight in the least.

One fall evening, Nathan had fulfilled all of his assigned duties and was sitting with Luke, a body servant who also served a master in the Holcombe Legion. Nathan and Luke had become close friends, something that Nathan had not really known on the plantation. Nathan had sometimes envied James for his friendship with Joseph, even though that friendship sometimes got him into trouble. Nathan could never find time to make close friends back home.

Nathan and Luke talked some about what was likely to happen the next day, then their conversation dwindled away to silence. Suddenly, Nathan's ears caught a faint sound, one which he had not heard in a long time.

He grabbed Luke's arm and whispered, "Did you hear dat noise?"

Luke said, "Don't know whut you be talkin bout. What did it sounds lik?"

"A rooster," responded Nathan, "Lik dem dat used to be round de Big House at home."

The two listened closely, then both heard it at the same time.

"Wat you say we sneak ober dar an see iffen we kin find him," suggested Luke.

"He be mitey fine eating tomorrow," said Nathan.

They talked strategy for a while and decided to wait a little longer, until it was completely dark. Unobserved, they crept out of camp in the general direction of the cock crow.

The men slithered over fences, around rock walls, all the while keeping a close eye and ear out for problems. They finally saw the farmhouse and out back, the chicken coop. The two whispered about the safest way to get into the chicken coop without disturbing human or canine residents of the farmhouse.

Nathan crept toward the chicken coop on his hands and knees, hoping the chickens had gone to sleep and he could nab a couple without awakening the others. Luke stayed back near the fence to keep watch. Nathan opened the door, trying not to let it squeak. He got inside, then almost closed the door. He waited until his eyes adjusted to the dark, then carefully reached into the first nest. His groping hand encountered a warm chicken, sleeping soundly on her eggs. He cracked his arm like a whip and snapped her neck. He reached for the next nest. Incredibly, his luck held, and he was able to dispatch the second hen and a third.

Then, greed took over, and he thought for a moment about a fourth. He carefully raised his head to eye level with the next nest, and to his great surprise, he looked eyeball to eyeball with another erstwhile thief--a red fox who was in the nest, looking for his own easy pickins. It was debatable as to which was the most startled, Nathan or Brer Fox. The fox gave a snarl, showing his teeth, then leaped off the nest and dashed out the door.

Nathan emitted a shriek, showing his own pearly white teeth, snatched up the three dead hens, and ran out the door, with the awful racket of a flock of rudely awakened chickens trailing behind him. The flock was short three members.

The next few minutes were a blur--Nathan and Luke ran as if the devil himself was behind them, over fences and walls. They heard the dogs raising cain and the boom of a shotgun tear through the night. These unwelcome sounds made them run all the harder, and they continued until they arrived safely back in camp. The next night, the two and their masters enjoyed the best meal since they had been in Charleston. The two masters really didn't question the body servants too closely as to where the entree had come from. For his part, Nathan opined that he had been mighty lucky in his foray, and he didn't try to liberate any other chickens from neighboring farmers. He had been lucky one time but might not be the next. The sound of that shotgun had gotten and kept his attention.

Master Will's regiment, the Holcombe Legion, had been assigned by Governor Pickens to guard the coastline of South Carolina. In Nathan's eyes, however, they seemed to spend most of their time running around in circles from one off-shore island to another, responding to rumors of the presence of Yankee invaders. Nathan became very proud of his Master, as Will's stock in the Legion grew. Will soon received a promotion to first lieutenant.

To Nathan thus far, war appeared to be a bunch of full-grown men playing games like children, much like he and his brothers played on the plantation before they were old enough to become field hands. That impression changed abruptly the day Master Will's unit came back from one of their forays and reported that they had skirmished with a large group of Yankees. They brought back several wounded men and the bodies of three soldiers killed in action. The soldiers of the Holcombe Legion had "seen the elephant" for the first time. Nathan, along with several other servants, was told to help the surgeon in cleaning up the dead and wounded, and Nathan had his baptism in blood. He realized the days of fun and games were over.

The soldiers of the Legion were saddened for quite a while, as most had been acquaintances in their days at the Citadel and had become good friends in the months near the coast in the Legion. The three soldiers killed in the skirmish were the first of them to go.

This subdued attitude disappeared a few days later when the rumor flew around camp that the Holcombe Legion had been called by General Robert E. Lee and their country. They were now part of the greater Confederate Army and would likely be moving out soon to fight in some place called Virginia.

Master Will rode over to the servants' camp early one morning and told Nathan to saddle his horse and fix his knapsack, as they had been given a surprise furlough for ten days. They were to return home to the plantation prior to their eminent departure toward northern Virginia and the joining with Lee's Army to face the massed Yankee armies there.

Nathan's heart pounded in his chest as he thought of seeing Momma and Stephen and James and of telling his family of all the adventures he had undergone and all of the sights he had seen. It was certain he had discovered a whole new world beyond the perimeter of the plantation.

The ride back home took one full day less than it had taken for them to get to Charleston. Nathan suspected that it was partially because he was much more comfortable on the horse than he had been on the first trip. He was able to worry more about riding and less about survival.

As they arrived at the plantation, Will dismounted at the Big House and said back over his shoulder, "Nathan, I'll see you in about four days. I suspect our lives are about to get much more difficult and dangerous than they've been. There are lots of Yankees up in northern Virginia where we're heading, and they'll be just as anxious to shoot us as we are them. But for now, forget about war and enjoy your furlough!"

Nathan responded, "We'll be fine, Massuh Will, we'll be fine! Afer all, weuns am de bes sojer and servant in de army!"

"All right," laughed Will, "we'll see! Now, get on home before your Momma thinks I've lost you to the fleshpots and gambling houses over in Charleston and comes after me with fire in her eye."

Nathan did as instructed and kicked his horse in the ribs. The horse snorted at the unexpectedly rough treatment, but broke into a gallop which did not stop until Nathan pulled him up in front of Momma's cabin. The cabin looked just as dilapidated as it ever had, with the weathered clapboard cracked and peeling in the hot South Carolina sun that penetrated the palmetto clearing, but to Nathan's heart, it was truly a palace. Momma came running out to see what or who was making such a commotion.

"Lordy, Lordy, its Nathan! Come here and gibs your Momma a hug! We had heared from de house girl dat you'uns wuz acomin back, but I didn't espect you dis fas!"

Nathan was engulfed in a smothering hug, given only as Momma could give.

"Whar am Stephen and James?" asked Nathan, when he regained his breath.

"Out in dat cotton field, dat's whar. Has you forgotten so fas dat dis here is plantin season?" responded Momma. "Dey will be along by and by. Dey bin lookin forwards tuh seein you. Dat's all dey bin talkin bout fer days! One ob de house girl's son bin hidin in de big tree in front ob de porch ob de Big House ever afternoon for days now, till Massuh Richard comes out tuh de porch wid a cigar after supper, and de boy bin listnin tuh de white folks talk. Dey lowed as how youuns would be back in a week or so. But here you am, now! Ize so happy." Momma began crying, big tears tracking down her face.

"Don't cry, Momma, be happy! Ize here, and Ize fine! Massuh Will says weuns will be here for bout four days afore we has tuh go back."

Momma said, "I is happy! Why does you tink Ize cryin?"

Nathan was saved from thinking any further about this example of inscrutable feminine logic by the timely arrival of James and Stephen.

"We wundered whose fine hoss dat wuz outside," shouted Stephen as he burst into the cabin. "We hoped it wuz yores!"

Stephen and Nathan embraced in a clumsy bear hug, with Nathan completely lifting his younger brother off his feet in his exuberance.

"How is you, James?" Nathan asked his brother, as they clasped forearms.

"Same as always, I reckon," responded James. "We works too hard in dat cotton field, we doesn't git enough tuh eat, and when we can't do all dat overseer wants, he threatens tuh whup us! I reckon you haz been gittin plenty tuh eat, along wid those fine clothes you is still wearin. You doesn't even look lik a slave no more."

Once again, as she had done so many times over the years, Momma interceded. "James, you hush dat jealous talk rite now! Be happy for yore brudder. Hush, and let's eat some supper. We kin talk after we eats. I wants to hear all bout Nathan's travels."

Nathan thoroughly enjoyed a supper which, for a change, he did not have to cook. He even managed to forget for a short time all of the new experiences which had happened to him over the months as he basked in the familiar glow of suppertime in the cabin. To Momma's amusement, Nathan asked questions about how many pinches or dashes of this or that Momma added to give her beans and cornbread their special flavor. He was serious about becoming a better cook to help him do his job as body servant. He also had to admit that he, to, was eating well and enjoying it. In these early days of the war, the Southern troops were still getting plenty of rations.

After Nathan and Stephen helped Momma with the dishes, she suggested that they all go outside to enjoy the cool breeze that was blowing for a change. They went outside and sat on several logs lying in the clearing near their home. The air wasn't quite so still and hot as it was in the cabin. Although he would never admit it out loud to anyone else, James was definitely curious to hear what Nathan had to say.

Finally, Momma burst out, "Well, Nathan, are you'uns gwine tuh make us wait all night, or are you gwine tell us what you bin doing? Where have de two of you bin sojerin?"

"Rite now, Ize jes enjoying bein wid ya'll," said Nathan. "But, I'll tell you everthin I members."

He launched into a description of everything he had been doing for the several months of absence. His interested audience of three gradually grew, as other slaves, curious about the story, drifted nearby and took seats on one of the logs. As his audience grew,

Nathan enjoyed more and more being the center of attention, and his stories became more complex and longer.

The audience oohed and ahed at the appropriate places, especially when Nathan told of helping clean up dead and wounded soldiers, preparing them for sending home for burial after the skirmish with the Yankees. Momma began fanning herself vigorously with her apron, and Nathan realized that he had perhaps better change the subject. He had saved what he felt was his best story for the finale.

"An, Massuh Will dun said dat he would git me my freedom at de end ob de fightin, iffen Ize a good body servant durin de war. I intends tuh do jest dat!"

Nathan sat back, extremely proud of his story telling, but to his amazement no one responded. Most of the slaves gradually drifted away in much the same manner that they had drifted in. It was later that Nathan realized that there was a touch of jealousy in the other slaves as he talked about being set free. He vowed to be more careful about whom he mentioned that to in the future.

"Nathan," James started after pondering his brother's words for a few minutes, "Ize proud dat iffen de Secesh wins and you does good, dat you will be free. De onliest problem I hab is, iffen de Secesh loses, den all ob us will be free! I wants you tuh be free, but I wants me and Stephen and Momma tuh be free, too! Ize confused; who does I wants tuh win? Iffen it looks lik de Secesh is gwine tuh win, den I haz tuh somehow git away from here. I jes knows I can't stands bein a slave no more!"

To James's complete surprise, he got no lecture about being a good slave, as Nathan thoughtfully rubbed his chin and responded, "I understand what you says, James. I wonders, tho, iffen you cuts and runs, what will dat overseer do tuh Momma and Stephen? I'm fraid he'll take it out on dem since he can't take it out on you. I worries bout dat."

"I don't tink he'll do anything tuh dem cause he tinks Ize such a bad apple. He won't blames dem."

Nathan thought about what James had said for a few more minutes, then said, "Let me thinks about dis for a while, little brudder. Meybe we kin talk more fore I has tuh go back tuh Charleston wid Massuh Will."

Momma, amazed at the mature and agreeable bond that had materialized between these two sons, led the way back to the cabin and a good night's sleep. The music of the spring peepers in the small wet-weather ponds in the lowlands plus the whip-poor-wills in the woods helped lull everyone to sleep. The music of the critters was as pretty as a lullaby played by the finest orchestra.

The first day of furlough was spent close to home, and Nathan was able to visit with James and Stephen in the fields and to talk more to Momma. He circulated amongst the other field hands and became a little depressed at the general mood and attitude those folks exhibited. He also realized that he now was a bit of an outsider, considered somewhat a traitor, as he was helping the Southern army. He was able to defend the situation by relating stories he had heard about how the free life for slaves that had run and attached themselves to Union forces wasn't really so hot, and the Yankees tended to use and abuse the runaways in a manner similar to the worst of the plantation overseerers.

Later that afternoon, a message came down from the Big House that Master Will wanted Nathan to accompany him to the neighboring plantation, as that owner wanted to talk with Will about how the war effort was going. Will also wanted to look at some mules that were for sale and wanted Nathan to help him drive them home. They were to leave tomorrow.

Early the next morning, Nathan and Will set out on the two mile ride, a distance that a year ago, would have been interminable to Nathan. When they arrived at the neighboring Big House, Will sat on the porch in an easy chair to visit with the owners, and Nathan went down to the barn to look at the livestock. The owner sent one of the house slaves, a young girl named Sadie, with Nathan. After one look at Sadie, Nathan became suddenly tongue tied, and his stammering re-appeared for the first time since he was a small boy.

As he walked toward the barn beside Sadie, Nathan stole a few sideways glances at her and declared to himself that she was for sure the prettiest thing he had ever laid eyes on, and he vowed to get to know her better. As they approached the barn door, he stole one last peek. He was amazed and disconcerted to see that she was stealing a glance at him! Both jerked their eyes back to the front, almost as if they had put their hands on a hot stove!

Sadie became a little bossy as she showed the young mules to Nathan, but he didn't mind that. As their conversation went on, his difficulty in talking abated, and he managed to steer the conversation on to other subjects, ranging from people they knew in common to his war experiences. They spent about an hour in the barn and finally did discuss the mules, four in all, that Sadie's owner desired to sell.

When Nathan and Sadie went back to the Big House, Nathan told Master Will that he thought the mules would be fine for wagon-pulling and other tasks around the plantation. Master Will took in the looks that Nathan was giving Sadie, much like a love-sick puppy, and smiled to himself. He thought, maybe I can help this situation somewhere down the line, but told Nathan, "Let's head home. It'll be tougher riding home, with each of us leading two of these contrary critters."

With one last look over his shoulder, Nathan sadly followed his master back to the plantation. Trying to lead the mules proved to be as difficult as Will had said, and accomplishing this while staying on his horse helped Nathan to forget Sadie, at least for a while.

Over the next few months, Will teased Nathan unmercifully, and Nathan could only say, "I declare, dat is surely de mos prettiest ting I ebber see. When de war am ober, I hopes I kin sees her again. I shore would lik to marry dat girl!"

Will said, "Maybe so, maybe so. I do know that if I need someone to run an errand to that plantation, I won't have any problem finding a volunteer!"

The next four days simply flew by. Nathan felt as though he had just arrived, when one of the house servants came by the cabin one evening and passed on Master Will's message that they were leaving on the morrow, and Nathan was to report to the Big House at dawn. His last day on furlough passed so fast it hardly felt like a full day. James asked a few more questions about life in the Charleston area, particularly in the few times that Nathan had been able to go into the city itself.

Stephen didn't say much at all, but instead just watched Nathan. His eyes followed his big brother as he moved about the cabin, packing his knapsack and preparing himself to go back to war. Supper was peaceful, and after all conversation ceased, the cabin fell quiet as darkness enveloped the palmetto woods and the slave-quarter clearing.

Early the next morning as Nathan made his final preparations, his family acted just as he thought they would. Momma cried, James grumbled, and Stephen was quiet. Nathan hugged all three of them, promised Momma he would be careful, and told Stephen to work hard to be the best field hand he could be.

He took James aside, out of Momma's hearing and said, "Little Brudder, I ain't forgot what you asked--I'll keep a'tinking bout it. But fer now, fer Gawd's sake, don't you rile dat overseer! Keep yore big mouf shut!"

James nodded his head in agreement, and Nathan felt better about James's attitude as he mounted his horse and rode up to the Big House. There he found the white folks saying goodbye in much the same way the slaves had.

Nathan and Master Will returned to Charleston, where they found that the promised trip to confront the Yankees in northern Virginia had been postponed for several weeks. Army camp life settled down into the same routine as before, almost as if they had never gone home on furlough.

Nathan's regular five-cent per pair of socks business flourished, as many soldiers had not gotten used to wearing dirty socks during

Nathan's absence. They welcomed his return with delight, and the ever-present pile of dirty socks again reappeared every morning. Nathan's business continued to grow and expand, and finally he was getting enough socks every day that he had to hire one of the other body servants to wash socks for him for two cents a pair.

☐ ☐ ☐ ☐

CHAPTER FIVE
THE HOME FOLKS' WAR
James
Fall, 1861 to Spring, 1862

At the Low Country plantation, the fall season cotton planting was completed. The slaves settled down to the back-breaking task of keeping weeds away from the young cotton plants. It seemed to James that those damned cotton plant stretched all the way to the horizon, and kept on going. He straightened up to rest his back for a moment and leaned on his hoe. He stared at the horizon with a "hundred-yard stare in a five yard space."

James's mind flashed back to what Nathan had said right before he rode away. I wonder if he really will help me, mused James, and he bent once again to chop weeds before the overseer noticed his daydreaming. Hot, humid days were endless, as the daily routine was broken only occasionally by the bits and pieces of war news which the slaves were able to overhear. James did as Nathan suggested, and he kept a low profile. He made sure he put on the "ole darky" routine for the overseer which kept the white folks happy, and which showed his "subservience".

The only time over this period of several months that he was tempted, really tempted, to show a flash of anger, was when he noticed that he had not seen his friend Joseph for several days. Asking around the slave compound, he found out from Old Ned that Joseph had been declared an incorrigible troublemaker. He had been sold to a plantation all the way across the state of South Carolina, in the Up Country.

James saw red for a moment at the treatment of his friend. He delayed action long enough to realize he could do Joseph no good by a temper explosion, and he certainly would bring problems on his own head. So, James opined that he was growing up, although this additional maturity made no difference in the way he felt about slavery in general, and his own slavery in particular.

Because of Nathan's absence, James took on the role of head of the household and helped Momma with chores many times before being asked. He kept the water bucket full, plenty of firewood in the bin, and he helped wash the dishes regularly, instead of going outside right after dinner to catch up on the day's news. Stephen helped as much as he could, but James found himself impatient at Stephen's slowness. He sometimes jumped in and completed tasks before Stephen could barely start.

When this happened, Stephen simply shook his head, looked at him sadly, and said, "James, I wuz doin dat; gib me enuf time."

James continuously circulated among his fellow field hands, trying to hear war news and what was likely to happen to the slaves. He was careful to note who was watching him in order to avoid getting the label of "troublemaker." That label always brought attention from the overseer; attention James was anxious to duck.

James got a rough idea of what was happening among the slaves on the other plantations in the Low Country. Some were causing considerable trouble for the plantation owners' wives left in charge, so their husbands could go off and fight. In most of those cases, the overseers returned the trouble to the slaves with substantial interest. More runaways were reported than before the start of the war; most of these were returned promptly, usually in the shape that Joseph was in when he was returned. James had heard of a few that had successfully made their way north, but these happy endings were few and far between.

James heard rumors of some entire slave families which had fled to the Sea Islands off the east coast of South Carolina. The slave who told him was somewhat prone to exaggeration, so James paid this story little mind. Some of the plantations had loaned or rented groups of slaves, mostly field hands, to the Confederate officials in charge of city defenses. The word through the slaves' grapevine was that those rented slaves had the worst time of all; they were required to perform hard labor of the most strenuous types, many times on substandard rations, rest, and medical attention.

The majority of slaves continued waiting and watching to see what would happen next. They daydreamed about what they would do if and when a decision was called for. Their home was nowhere near any of the war action yet and slave unrest always occurred nearer the action.

James saw less and less of the white folks from the Big House. The ladies, Miss Annie and her daughters, used to come down to the slave cabins on holidays, bringing special goodies for the men and cast-off fancy clothes for the female slaves; clothes which those ladies then proudly wore to church on Sunday. The word among the slaves was that, the white folks were maybe just a little bit afraid of their own slaves! James had a problem swallowing that explanation.

Old Master Richard and that trash overseer were very much still in charge, and the overseer used the whip even more than before the war began to impact the way things were done on the plantation. However, he was careful to avoid using that whip when someone was present from the Big House.

Oh well, thought James, no rush! Let things happen as they happen, then when the time is right, just watch James! I may decide to be away from here in a flash, that's what! If Joseph can almost get away, I may be able to succeed. But for now, Momma and Stephen need my help, so I reckon I'll stick around for a while and help them.

Things moved along at a slow pace much like before the war, and fall became winter, and winter became spring.

Early in the spring, the word came down from the Big House late one evening, "Old Massuh Richard's sickly! He be real sickly. He can't eben talk or eat. Dey fraid he gwine die!" This word came from one of the house servants, who happened to be passing close by the cabins of the field hands while on an errand. A current of fear of the unknown spread like a cold fog in the early evening that moved as if alive.

Several days later, the word was passed around the plantation that Master Richard had died. All of the slaves were expected to put on their Sunday best and pay their respects the following day up at the Big House.

A greater fear than ever spread among the slaves as to what might happen since Old Master Richard was gone. They obeyed their orders and presented themselves at the Big House for the wake and funeral. They lived in fear the plantation might be closed or sold, and themselves along with it. Even though they hated slavery, they knew that they had it fairly easy because many of them had talked with slaves from other plantations. Master Richard and Miss Annie treated them well and actually treated them more as people than as livestock. In fact, Joseph was the only slave sold off that plantation for many years, and even the most dissident of the slaves had to admit that Joseph had been a troublemaker.

The slaves performed on funeral day as required, with the obligatory tears and wails "'bout pore, pore Massuh." James and Stephen and most of the field hands got their first look at the parlor of the Big House.

As James looked around at the parlor where Master Richard was laid out, he thought to himself, "I reckon that all of the slave quarter cabins would fit together in this one room!"

Old Master Richard was laid to rest in the family cemetery, located on the crest of one of the few hills on the plantation, behind the Big House.

Following the service, Mistress Annie asked for all the slaves, field hands and house servants alike, to gather at the front porch, so she might speak to them. Fear surfaced among the slaves, as they speculated on the worst that could occur. Would Mistress Annie decide to sell them? Were families about to be divided? There was nothing to do but stand and wait for the dreaded words.

When they were in place, she started, "I wanted to thank you all for your expressions of sorrow for Master Richard. Now, I need to ask for your help to continue to run this plantation. Just before he was stricken ill, he told me that the Confederate government in Richmond passed a law that will require all plantations to plant more corn and wheat and less cotton. We're having trouble selling the cotton anyway, so I guess that's all right. This week, we'll start clearing more of the bottom land to grow additional corn. This will be new to all of us, so I need your help. Again, I thank you for your loyalty to us."

She went inside and the relief was evident on the faces of all the slaves. They left the Big House and scattered to their respective cabins, reflecting on what Miss Anna had said.

James thought to himself, I reckon that the trouble will soon begin, now! We'll see if Missy and that trash overseer can control one hundred slaves, or whether a hundred slaves will control the white folks.

Even after all of the excitement, life on the plantation slowed back down to a humdrum, sweaty, wearying existence. Corn planting on the newly cleared bottom land added a little bit of spice. James and the other field hands enjoyed watching the overseer direct them in a task which he had never done himself, sweating as much as them in the process. They managed to keep straight faces.

Somehow, the planting was accomplished. Unfortunately, James and Stephen and their brother and sister field hands discovered as young crops came up, hoeing of the voracious weeds was equally tough whether the desired crop was cotton, corn, or whatever! The sun was just as hot, sweat stung your eyes just as badly, the hoe got just as heavy by the end of the day, and your back hurt just as much come nightfall. The novelty of the new crop wore off.

James worked even harder at keeping his mouth shut and at doing more than his share at helping Momma with the chores. At the same time, however, he continued to keep his ear to the rumor mill which was not only present among the slaves on their plantation and neighboring plantations, but gave every indication of becoming more timely and accurate every day of the conflict. At this point in the war, the South was doing well and had whipped the North at a number of battles.

In fact, a house boys overheard one of the neighbor men who was there to check on Miss Annie say, "I swear, if I really want to know what is going on either on the warfront or on any plantation in the Low Country, all I have to do is to listen to my slaves. My niggers are more up-to-date than I am! I even snuck down to the slave cabins the other night and crawled underneath one of them and listened to the talk going on. It sure told me which of the niggers I need to watch for signs of trouble."

When James heard this, he panicked for a minute, as he thought back to some of the conversations he had been involved in during the past few months. Then he calmed down as he remembered that most discussions had been held out in the woods rather than in cabins. Nevertheless, he resolved to take extreme care in the future, particularly when a discussion turned to topics which the white folks were likely to find objectionable or seditious in nature. He had learned that what the white folks found objectionable soon found its way back to the slaves in the form of painful retribution. A closed mouth equaled fewer problems from the overseer, and fewer problems with the overseer was a goal worth working for.

Several days later, one of the field hands said something that offended the overseer and he exploded. He knocked the slave down with the butt of the whip, bloodying his nose, and nearly closing one eye with the single blow. As the slave lay on the ground, the overseer picked up his coiled blacksnake whip, stretched it out and started methodically beating the slave, beginning on his feet and moving up his body. The crack of the whip and the screams of the slave filled everyone's ears and senses.

James clenched his hands until his fingernails cut into his palms and made them bleed. He wanted to jump in and help the man but was certain of the consequences of such an action. Then, almost as if in answer to an unsaid prayer, James heard the sound of a horse, and Miss Annie rode into the field. She screamed at the overseer, and he stopped beating the slave.

"What are you doing," she asked.

"This Negra back talked me, and I was jest teaching him some respect for his betters," the overseer panted.

"You've taught your last lesson here," replied Miss Annie. "Go get your things and get off this plantation before nightfall."

He snarled, "Jest how do you intend tuh run this place without me tuh keep these niggahs under control?"

She answered, "That's not your problem anymore. Now, leave, before I go get the sheriff to make you leave."

He slunk away in the direction of his cabin.

Annie turned to James and said, "Get someone to help you carry this man up to the Big House, and tell my housekeeper to get him into bed and to send someone after the doctor. I told that overseer and my husband told him before he died that we simply do not treat our slaves in that way, and he just wouldn't listen."

She turned to another slave and told him to go hide in the woods and watch the overseer as he packed his belongings and to report back to her when he had gone.

James did as he was told, and he and another field hand carried the beaten man to the Big House, as gently as possible. The piteous moans made James remember how much the one stripe he had received from the overseer's whip had hurt, and this poor man had received some ten fold in pain and agony. Several hours later, after the white doctor had come and gone, James returned to his cabin to tell Momma the latest happenings. The emotions of the field hands were increased even more by the uncertainties of the work in the fields tomorrow, without an overseer.

The next day, no one came down from the Big House early in the morning, and the field hands faced a real dilemma. There was no longer an overseer, and the temptation to take a day off was great. James thought once again about what Nathan had preached over and over, and he picked up his hoe. He started walking in the direction of the corn field, taking his time.

As James walked, he glanced back over his shoulder. Stephen was right behind him, and to his surprise, the other field hands, without a word, followed their lead. They reached the field and began the day's work. The work progressed as well as if there were supervision present. At lunch time, Miss Annie and two of her daughters rode to the field in the wagon and brought the field hands water and a lunch of cornpone and fatback, just as if it were a normal workday.

Miss Annie stopped by James's side as she and the girls were preparing to leave and said in a quiet voice, "James, I understand that it was you and Stephen who led the others out here to work today, and I wanted to thank you. I'm starting to look for a new overseer, but good men are tough to find with the war. I'll be careful as to whom I hire. I need you to keep on working as you have. We must provide foodstuffs for our boys out on the battlefields."

She left, and James had even more conflicting thoughts. He was violently opposed to aiding and abetting the war, because he believed the South was fighting to keep all colored people in slavery. Yet, here he was, helping the South! Miss Annie's thank-you had felt good, but the mixed emotions were difficult to sort out. For now, he would continue as he had been doing, and be prepared to react to whatever came his way.

James glanced at Stephen and for a moment he wished they could change places. Life was not complex for Stephen. He was capable of shutting down his thought processes and plodding in a straight line without worrying. On the other hand, James felt that he had more worrying and thinking to do than he had ever had before, and his mind was as tired at the end of the long day as his back. As head of the household, he had more chores that had to be done. It was easier to go ahead and do them than to kick in the traces like a stubborn mule. So, James just did what he had to do.

Over the next few weeks, the situation did not change in the least. Miss Annie and the girls continued to bring food and water to the field hands every day at noon, and the slaves kept on doing their work. Several slaves slacked off as soon as the wagon creaked and rattled out of sight. The lazy ones were called down by one of the hard-working hands as making their own jobs tougher. No one objected to doing their part of the work, but they resented one who made more work for them by loafing. No new overseer appeared on the scene, but on several occasions, neighboring plantation owners came down to the fields accompanying Miss Annie at lunch time, apparently to help her keep track of progress. They were amazed at what they saw during the visits.

James overheard one of the men say to Miss Annie, "I sure wish my niggers worked like yours. My overseer is pretty tough on them, but they show respect for us only because of that. We've noticed that they slow down their work when we're not around; yours have no overseer, yet they keep on working."

James strained his ears to hear Miss Annie's response but couldn't. He spent the rest of the afternoon pondering the man's comments. He again felt a little spark of pride, and the thought crept into his head that, maybe, just maybe, if the situation continued as it was and they gave Miss Annie no reason why she had to have an overseer, the field hands might not have to deal with that unpleasant situation. He swore to himself to work harder than ever and he would make sure the other field hands did the same. He would use whatever it took to show Miss Annie they were dependable. Hope springs eternal in the human breast!

CHAPTER SIX
FLIGHT
James
Spring, 1862

James's complacency came to a sudden and breathtaking halt late one warm, sultry night. At about two o'clock in the morning, he was awakened from a deep sleep when his shoulder was vigorously shaken.

"Who dat," he croaked?

"Iz jes me," replied a voice he recognized as belonging to Joseph, his former fellow slave who had been sold months ago to a plantation on the other side of the Low Country.

Joseph was standing just outside the window, leaning on the windowsill in James's corner of the cabin.

"What you doin here, Joseph? Iz you is trubble?"

"I reckon I iz," Joseph replied. "I dun run away. Ize now free, dat's what Ize!"

"Whar is you goin?" asked James.

"Ize gwine tuh join de Fus Souf ober on Sea Islands, dat's what Ize gwine do. De Fus Souf fights de Secesh for they freedom; Ize gwine hep. Come wit me, boy, an you'll be free, too!"

James fell back into his mussed, sweaty pallet. Now his mind was really whirling! This could be his answer. Freedom, and at the same time, to be able to fight for the freedom of all the slaves he knew! He squirmed uncomfortably as he thought of any possible problems.

"I heared ob some slaves gwine tuh de Sea Islands, but I thoughts dat de man who telled me dat wuz lying. Who is in de Fus Souf, Joseph? Am dar anybudy we knows? I dun heared ob dat army, but I don't know nuttin bout dem," questioned James from his reclined position.

Joseph responded, "De Fus Souf is nuttin but men who used to be slaves. De officers are all white Yankee officers--dey learns us how tuh fight and gibs us guns, so we kin kill Secesh. No mo time tuh talks now. We gotta git a long ways befo daylight."

James had to make the quickest decision of his life. He had not thought that this time of decision would come so quickly, or be so tough when it did come. James made up his mind. "Wait, Joseph. I'm a'comin wid you, but I needs tuh tells Momma whar Ize goin. Oderwise, she be worried bout me."

"No," hissed Joseph. "We can't tells nobuddy. Iffn you tells her, de buckras will beat it out ob her, an you don't wants dat!"

"Youze right," said James, "I don't wants dat!"

James threw his clothes and his few possessions into a gunny sack. He stealthily crept into the main part of the cabin, grabbed the remnants of last night's dinner, and tossed that into his sack on top of his clothes. The two men shouldered their loads and in silence, crept out into the dark, oppressive South Carolina night.

They left their former lives behind without a single glance back and headed toward some adventure or another. They had no idea what that adventure would either be or bring, but both felt in their hearts that it had to be better than slavery. James had gotten some pride in his temporary role as overseer of the field hands and their work, but he was afraid that situation could change any day.

James and Joseph managed to walk and run eight miles during the rest of that night. The moon was almost full, so the countryside was bright--bright enough that they could see where they were stepping. Unfortunately, it was also light enough that they felt as if anyone could see them, even from a distance. The walking off-road in this part of South Carolina was relatively easy. The countryside consisted of alternating palmetto forests and cultivated fields and they walked for the most part in the woods lining the dirt roads in the moonlight.

Several times they had to change directions, as they caught sight of plantation lights. On one frightening occasion, the hunting dogs from a plantation began barking, and James's heart lurched further up in his chest than he thought possible.

The men scurried back into the palmettos and through the high grasses and left the sound of the hounds behind. James and Joseph ran at what felt like full-tilt for about a mile, enough distance that they felt safe temporarily from pursuit. They fell on the ground at the base of a large tree covered with long, creepy Spanish Moss and panted much like large dogs themselves. Their pounding pulses slowly returned to normal.

"Dat wuz close," breathed James.

"Yeah, I wuz fraid fer a minute dat it wuz de dog company," said Joseph. "I heared bout dem from one ob de slaves at dat plantation dey sold me tuh. Dey am bunches ob Secesh sojers dat trabbels round wid hounds lookin for runaways. Dey ketches dem an returns dem tuh dey massuhs. Dey plenty rough, dat's what I hears. Dey am worser dan eny overseer."

James said, "We couldn't talk at my cabin bout de Fus Souf--do we hab time now?"

"I reckon so," said Joseph. "It am mitely near dawn--We best find a better hole in dese woods tuh hide fer de day. Let's gwine, an we kin talks quiet, eben though I doesn't knows much more dan I already tells you."

The men crept deeper into the woods. They startled a deer, a large doe, who had been resting in a thicket of vines in the palmettos. After James and Joseph recovered from their own scare, they decided that if the spot was good enough for the deer to hide from hunters, it was also good enough for the men to hide from their almost certain pursuers. The men settled in to sleep for the day. Before James could even begin with his questions, both men fell into a deep sleep.

It was late afternoon before they stirred again. It was the hottest part of the day and the sweat oozed from every pore in their bodies and the loud, protesting grumbling of their empty bellies echoed through the thicket. Even when exhausted, it is difficult to sleep when you are wringing wet and your belly sounds like someone beating on the plantation wagon wheel.

James broke the piece of stale, hard cornbread he brought from home and gave part of it to Joseph.

"Ain't much, but better nuttin," James said.

The men devoured every crumb, then drank with their hands from a small puddle of water within the clearing.

"Now, Joseph," said James, "Tells me whut you knows bout dis Fus Souf."

"Don't knows much," began Joseph, "Ceptin dat dey officers am all Yankees and dey is out on Sea Island, below Charleston. It ain't easy tuh git out dar, an we'll hab tuh steal a boat and row neath de Secesh noses. Iffen dey ketch us it am back tuh slavery, complete wid beatin, iffen dey don kills us fus. Once we git out dar, we'll jine up an be sojers."

"I heard dat de Yankees mite sells us tuh Cuba fer slaves an dey am meaner dan de white buckras dat owns us now, dat's what de overseer say," worried James.

"Dat's jest what he say tuh keep you from runnin," responded Joseph. "Dey don't do dat!"

The two men retreated into their own thoughts and waited, not so patiently, for dusk, then complete darkness. The afternoon and evening turned cloudy and the moon was barely visible through the clouds. The night symphony began, with songs of the courting frogs blending with those of the whip-poor-will and the mourning dove. At times, the music was so loud, it was hard to even think, much less hear anyone or have them hear you.

"Dat's good," exclaimed Joseph, "We'll be able tuh move much faster, and dey won't be able tuh see us cause it be darker dan las night. I believes dat de song of de critters am even louder dan dey was las nite. We should be able to covers a lots o ground. Pick up yore tote sack and let's go! Cause we don know whar de Firs Souf am, it mite takes us a long time to find em!"

The two men began the second evening of their perilous journey, half-walking and half-jogging to make better time. To their relief, the entire night passed with no contact with people, black or white. Just as dawn began to break, the men started searching for a hiding place where they could catch some much-needed rest.

As they passed into a palmetto copse, they literally ran into a man in the faint early light of day. The man was knocked down and James fell on top of him, but he started struggling and attempted to yell. James and Joseph subdued him and James clapped a none-to-gentle hand over his mouth.

"Look, Joseph, he am one ob us!" exclaimed James.

He bent down to the man and whispered, "Is you all through tryin tuh yell? Will you'un be quiet iffin I turns you loose?" The man, whose eyes were about the size of Momma's cornbread skillet, vigorously nodded his head affirmatively, and James released him. The three men stood up and dusted the Carolina sand off their clothes.

"What is you crazy niggers doing here, anyway?" queried the stranger.

"We is runnin away tuh join de Fus Souf army and fight de Secesh," explained James.

"You fight him as good as you fight me, you do all right," said the man. He shook his head in disbelief. "You damn near kilt me, dat's fer sartin sho. Dey is some Secesh in dis area. De dog company am on de nex plantation. You will hab tuh be some mighty kerful. I kin tells you a safe way to go fer de nex few miles. Dat mite helps a bit. You two gots eny food?"

"No," said Joseph, "Kin you git us eny?"

"Maybe I kin git some corn pone and a bit ob fatback," replied the man.

"We precciate it, fer sho," said Joseph. "We be rite here, in dis here grove for de day, hidin from de dog sojers. When you kin, bring de food, cause we be mitey hongry. Don't tells nobody bout us being here, else we git caught for sho."

The man turned to leave, and said back over his shoulder, "Be back later wid some foods. Don't move around none, or dey ketch you fer sartin."

In hushed tones, James and Joseph discussed whether or not they could trust the slave. Deciding that they had no real choice, they used their hands to scoop out hollows to serve as beds in the sand. They collapsed into exhausted sleep.

True to his word, at dusk some 12 hours later, the slave returned to the grove, startling the boys into wide-awake readiness. To save a repetition of yesterday's struggle, the man hurriedly reassured them that he was a friend. He carried a small sack containing scraps of food and a small water bottle.

"Dat's all I could gits," said the man. "Hope dat helps some."

"For sartin," said James as he tore into a piece of cornbread. "We preciate it; least now we won't starve fer a bit, enyway."

The man turned to leave the clearing, but came back and said, "I surely would like tuh come wit you boys, but Ize too old, and my woman needs me here. Fight good fer us, too!"

He waved his hand, and turned to walk back to the fields of the plantation where he lived and worked. The two runaways finished their paltry meal as if it were the finest prime rib in the best restaurant in Charleston. Feeling stronger, they packed up their gunny sacks, and started, as darkness had fallen. Happily, once again, it had fallen their lot to be blessed with an almost moonless night, and they made substantial progress in their journey.

☐ ☐ ☐ ☐

CHAPTER SEVEN
THEN THERE WAS ONE
Stephen
Spring, 1862

The morning James had finally run away, Momma woke to find his bed had been slept in but was now cold.

She roughly shook Stephen's shoulder, and told him, "Stephen! I can't finds James--run ober tuh de spring, den by de barn, and see iffen you kin finds him. I hope he ain't dun nuttin dumb, but Ize afraid dat he haz! Now, git, fore de white folk am up and aroun!"

Stephen, still groggy from his night's sleep, jumped out of bed and managed to stick both feet into the same trouser leg. He fell hard to the dirt floor of the cabin. He picked himself up and started over again. This time he had only one of his legs per pants leg, so he made a dash through the dusky dawn. He started looking in the places Momma had suggested he look for his older brother and he tried a few more possible places.

Fifteen or twenty minutes later, he returned, completely out of breath. He managed to vigorously shake his head and breathlessly say, "No, Momma, he iz not in enny of dem places."

"Lordy, Lordy, I reckon dat boy has finally run away. What's we gwine do, now? Fus I loses Nathan to de war, now James to Gawd knows whut. What's I gwine do?" wailed Momma.

Stephen replied, "I reckons we mus kiver for him, bes we kin. It be better dat he git away than dey brings him back beat half to death. We has tuh hope dat dey won't beat us half tuh death, as well!" Stephen put his arms around Momma. He said, "Momma, at leas you haz me an I ain't gwine nowhere—youze stuck wid me."

Momma's jaw dropped as her youngest son spoke his mind for one of the few times she could remember.

"Momma," Stephen said, "Don't looks at me lik one ob us has lost dey mind. I always bin able tuh talk fer myself, but it's jes dat Nathan and James always haz plenty tuh say, so I jes keeps quiet. Now, as I say, we has tuh keep it quiet so James gits as much distance tween he and dem hounds as he kin. Heps me tuh fix his bed."

The two placed some unused bedding and an old pillow in James's pallet and plumped it up making it look as much as possible that it still contained its former occupant. Stephen went to the tool shed and shouldered his hoe. He started walking slowly toward the field in which they had worked yesterday. Several of the other field hands came out of their cabins just as Stephen started. They, like him, picked up their tools and purposefully headed out towards their day's work. The situation looked much like normal, exactly what Stephen hoped for.

By half way through the morning, several of the field hands had asked Stephen where James was.

He curtly responded, "He be sick in de bed, dat's whar he be. I reckon he may be better tomorrow—iffn he is, he'll be here."

At noontime when Miss Annie and the girls brought the hands' food, she, too, questioned Stephen. She gave every indication of accepting Stephen's response, and the rest of the day went without any problems.

Stephen and the rest of the hands went home at dusk. As per usual, he washed up good at the spring. He stuck his head down into the spring pool for a second, then shook the excess water off of his face and hair, as if he was trying to wash off scared thoughts in addition to dust. Momma had not been able to leave the fields early as she normally did, so the two shared a cold dinner, but very few words. They went to bed early, wondering if James was all right and where he might be at that time. The next morning, Stephen went back to the field and began work.

At mid-morning, Miss Annie rode into the field, leaving a trail of dust. She reigned her mare to a sudden stop. She was accompanied by one of her neighbors. He had been one of those checking on the slaves following Master Richard's death.

"You, boy," shouted the man at Stephen. "Where is your brother, you worthless nigger?"

"He be at home sick--I seen him under de cubbers dis mornin," Stephen stammered.

"You're lying! He's not thar!" shouted the man. "We just checked, and those were clothes under his covers, not him!" He drew out his whip from behind him on the saddle. "I'll get the answer out of you!"

Miss Annie reached out and stopped him. "We don't use the whip on this plantation, Charles. I guess I know that James has run. I thought he was one of our better hands, and maybe I trusted him too much. Do you know if any of the Confederate patrols in charge of runaways are in the area?"

The man thought for a moment, then said, "I reckon I heard tell of the dog patrol being over on the other side of the county. Let me send my overseer over there to get them, and they'll bring back that nigger, quick enough, I promise you that."

The two reined their horses about in a tight circle and rode hurriedly back toward the Big House. Stephen gulped a gasping breath. He was pleased at the lack of retribution against him and Momma. He also couldn't decide whether to be prouder that they had given James a day-and-a-half head start, or to worry more what would happen when and if they caught up with James, wherever it was he had run to.

While pondering these thoughts, Stephen bent again to the task of hoeing the weeds from around the young corn plants. He tried to blank his mind, as he normally did with so much success, but was not even able to do that. His mind kept working on possibilities and he projected future events. Somehow, the day slowly dragged to a torturous close, and he hurried back to the cabin, afraid of what he would find. To his relief, Momma was there as usual, preparing dinner.

He rushed in, and panted, "Momma, you iz all right!"

"'Course I is. Ize fixin dinner, as always. Did you wash yore hands at de spring?" She caught his hands, looked at them, and said, "Git on back dere an wash yore hands and face and behind yore ears. You knows we alays do dat afore we eats!"

Stephen flashed a grin from ear to ear, and turned to run back to the spring for washing. Somehow he felt as long as Momma was still acting like Momma, things would be all right. He returned to the cabin, and the cornbread and fatback and beans meal for the two passed without incident.

"You ain't plannin tuh do somethin dumb like James, is you?" Momma asked.

Stephen thought for a moment and responded, "No, Momma, I telled you, I reckons I'll stay here an hep you as de man ob de house. Way I sees it, dis war can't las forebber. Whan it be ober, den we kin see whut we needs to do. No, I ain't gwine run, quit worrin bout dat—I'll be here."

Momma smiled at him, and said, "I reckon you'll do jes fine as de man ob de house. Let's us pray tuh de Lor dat James don't git caught or killed by dem dog soldiers."

The two, mother and son, went to their respective corners of the cabin, and fell to their knees in prayer. As full darkness descended over the Low Country, sleep descended, just as fully. When Stephen rose the next day and prepared to go to the fields to work, he felt rested like he hadn't felt for a long time.

Stephen and Momma went through the next few days almost as if sleepwalking. They continuously checked with the house servants to see if anything had been heard about James and his whereabouts or condition. They found out absolutely nothing. The constant concern dissipated as time passed, as it appeared that James had made a successful escape to wherever he was running. So, once again, life settled down to a humdrum existence. Stephen, facing no older sibling pressures, almost seemed to flower daily, taking more and more charge of the work being conducted by the other field hands.

Old Ned, though recognized as one of the leaders of the field hand community, watched Stephen's progress and allowed him to take charge.

Miss Annie and the girls continued to visit the fields at lunch time. Several times, Stephen noticed Miss Annie watching him as he cautiously took charge, settled arguments, and kept tasks lined up for the hands. Clearly, the field hands noticed that no new overseer had been hired, a situation which was thoroughly enjoyed by all. The slaves, including the older ones, allowed Stephen to continue taking charge, and Stephen reminded them of that on a regular basis. He reasoned that if they continued to work hard and stay out of trouble, Miss Annie might not feel she needed a white field hand overseer. That was something the field hands worked hard to keep as it was, and they would keep on working like they were for as long as they could. So, Stephen was an overseer by silent vote.

Several days later, word came to Momma through the house servant to field servant communications chain, that James had been seen with Joseph near a plantation several counties east of their own plantation. After they recovered from their surprise to discover that Joseph had re-surfaced, they were equally pleased that the two men were well, at least at that time. It was also rumored that the men were heading for the Charleston area to fight for a Yankee outfit. Stephen and Momma hoped the white folks' communications was not as good as their own, as certain retribution would follow if the folks in the Big House learned of James's intentions.

It proved that the white communication was not as good, as nothing was said by Miss Annie. She also spent more and more time with Stephen, asking him questions about what he felt needed to be done next. They discussed how to best harvest the corn, which was near-ripe. Miss Annie and Stephen decided to pick the corn ears in much the same way that they picked the cotton, with the corn tossed into a bag slung across the shoulder of each field hand. The filled bags were to be collected, tossed into the collecting wagon, and replaced with a new bag at the end of each row completed.

In this way, the first corn harvest from the plantation was completed, and both owners and hands felt a semblance of pride. The crop was taken to town where part was sold to help with plantation expenses, which were rapidly rising as the value of the Confederate dollar continued to slowly sink. The rest of the corn crop was conscripted for the ever-increasing feeding needs of the Confederate Army. The unfortunate dichotomy was produced by inflation resulting from the new Southern government buying more food, supplies, armament and gunpowder with money whose value was going in the opposite direction from the needs of the army.

CHAPTER EIGHT
THE FLIGHT CONTINUES
James
Spring, 1862

During this time, the situation for the runaways became more and more difficult and harrowing. In order to avoid plantations that were more closely located as they drew nearer to Charleston, they had to move into and through the swamps. To now, they had managed to avoid the actual swamps, although they had walked beside many on their travels. Each step into the black, rotting masses of leaves and vegetation on the bottom of the swamp released clouds of stinking sulfur gasses that made breathing painful and even nigh-impossible. This made the travel more difficult, particularly when the men encountered high swamp grass which could cut you like a knife, if you weren't careful.

James and Joseph saw more mud and mosquitoes than they cared for or even knew existed. Once, they accidentally walked very close to a large black cottonmouth snake. The snake was as thick as a man's arm and was sunning on the bank. This caused great fear and consternation and the two moved much more carefully, once their heart beats slowed down and their trembling limbs functioned again.

The men had several close calls with men and dogs as the Dog Soldiers were more frequent in this part of the Low Country, the closer they came to Charleston. The Confederates realized early in the war that the Sea Islands area would be a real problem to them when the Yankees took control of that part of South Carolina. They didn't realize that it would become a Garden of Eden to runaway slaves or allow the setting up of regiments of black soldiers with white officers to lead them, but that was exactly what happened.

Late one night, just before dawn and their obligatory sleep stop until dusk, the runaways heard a faint noise; they stopped dead in their tracks, trying to determine the source of the noise. Joseph turned around in the nick of time to barely see a large bloodhound growling deep and charging in their direction.

He whispered loudly, "James, James!" James picked up a small log and caught the dog beside the head as he projected himself upwards at Joseph's throat. The dog gave one whimper and James struck him again and again. The dog lay still.

"Dere," said James, "I hated tuh do dat but dat's one less helper de Dog Sojers has tuh ketch us. I hope dat de sojers dat am wit dat dog am far away! I believes dat iffen I had de choice, I'd sooner face dat cotton snake we seed dan de Dog Sojers."

James and Joseph continued to slog through the swamps. Happily, the soldiers which were using the dog they had killed either were nowhere near or they simply did not notice the loss of their dog in time to hunt down the runaways. The men continued their journey suffering no further such frightening incidents, at least for the time being. They found a safe hummock in the swamp where they were able to curl up and sleep fitfully for the day, during those times when the blood-thirsty mosquitoes ceased their attacks. James swore that the mosquitoes saved up their energy for every fresh attack and he could hear them as they circled, ready to swoop.

The next day at dusk, they choked down the remnants of their dry cornbread. Joseph announced, "James, I thinks we am not far from de wide ribbers dat am near de Sea Islands. Meybe we not have any more probbems. We haz tuh look for a boat dat we kin use in gittin ober tuh de Sea Islands."

James plaintively said, "I hopes we kin find dat boat, cause I don't tink Ize kin swim. We splash in de shallow pond when we wuz little, but nebber swim. Iffn dose ribbers be as wide as you bin a'tellin me, weze gwine hab to swim!"

Joseph said, "I thinks we kin find a fishin boat belong tuh some pore cracker. De older de better, so he won't miss it fer a long time. We kin row under de Secesh noses an git ober tuh de islands. Den we finds de Fus Souf and den we be all right."

The two set out for what they hoped would be their last night's journey by foot. Just before daylight was breaking, they crept out of the dark, swampy woods onto the shore of an extremely wide estuary river. The river contained more water than either of them had ever seen in their lives, and they paused, open-mouthed, with pounding chests. When they looked around, they saw a scene that was almost spooky. The large oaks had massive branches that trailed just about to the ground and Spanish Moss hung from every possible toehold on the branches. The swamps and mud were still present on either side of the high point on the bank where they stood, but at least their feet were dry. The water of the estuary looked sluggish and was dark green in color.

James reached down and cupped his hand in the water and took a mouthful. He spat it out and exclaimed, "Damn, dat water gots salt in it! I nebber hearded of sech a ting!"

Joseph laughed. "I heared dat de ocean has salt in it—I guess we be close enuff to de ocean dat dis water am salty too."

James looked at the estuary again with wide eyes and moaned, "Lordy, iffen we don find dat boat, my freedom am ober fore it begin. I can't wade or swim dat water, dat's fer sartain sho. I'll haz to sit on dis ribber bank till de dog sojers come and ketch me or a cotton snake kill me."

Joseph replied, "I tolds yuh tuh not worry; we finds a boat, steals it, den row quiet tuh de Sea Islands. Den we be free an fights de Secesh!"

The two men gambled with daybreak rapidly coming and they searched in the bushes growing profusely on the banks of the river. Just as light was winning its struggle with the night, James stubbed his toe and sat down on the muddy bank of the estuary. Swearing vigorously, he sat up, rubbing his throbbing bare toe.

"Dat hurt lik de debbil," he growled. "What did I hit, ennyway?"

He stood up and brushed off the mud. He limped over and pushed aside the bushes where he sat. To his utter amazement, there was a small wooden boat containing one old warped, cracked oar. The boat had a couple of small obvious holes near the bow. As the two excited men closely examined the craft, they figured it could be repaired well enough to make their way down the river, by the Confederate fort, and on to the Sea Islands. James suggested that they drag it to a safe resting place and work on it during the day light while it was impossible for them to move about.

"No, no," exclaimed Joseph. "We can't do dat. Iffen we drags dat boat, sumbudy libble tuh come by today, and follow de marks in de sand. We haz tuh wait, hard as it be."

The two men re-covered the boat with brush and moved with care back into the deep bushes and woods. They drug a fallen palmetto branch behind them to erase their footprints in the sand. Resting during that day was difficult, the most difficult of their entire journey. The men lay side by side and excitedly whispered about how to repair the boat. James spent another hour scraping a branch to serve as a second oar. Finally exhausted, he fell asleep and joined Joseph, who had given up the battle to remain awake some time earlier.

Come dusk, James and Joseph crept back to the old boat and drug it out of the heavy bush cover. They carefully examined it from bow to stern. Although the boat looked even more decrepit in the rapidly dimming light of this day, at least most of the wood appeared to be sound and the dry rot had not yet consumed the planking or the ribs. To their relief, the two small holes they had found the evening before in the bow appeared to be the only structural damage. They scraped small pieces of wood and carefully fitted them into the holes, after binding the plugs with scraps of what was left of their tattered shirts.

They stepped back to admire their handiwork, and Joseph said, "Ize you ready, James?"

James teeth chattered with excitement and with fear. "I guess so. Ize ready as I ebber will be. I hopes dat dis boat holds us up out ob dat evil water."

The men struggled to drag the boat to the water's edge, and launched it. They crawled in and pushed off from the bank, suffering substantial trepidation. They put their makeshift oars in place and began rowing.

The boat had moved only about one hundred feet from the shore when James exclaimed, "Joseph! My feet am gittin wet!" Dis boat leak all ober!"

Joseph looked down and saw water bubbling from every single crack between pairs of planks. His eyes opened as wide as James's and the two turned the boat and frantically began rowing back toward the shore.

Before they had gone thirty feet, the boat gunnels were level with the water, and James cried out, "Joseph, Ize gwine drown! I telled yuh I couldn't swim a lick!"

Joseph was suffering a similar panic attack. He slipped out of the boat and into the water. He held on to the gunwale with a death grip. He surprised James as he began laughing so vigorously that tears ran down his cheeks.

"What is you laughin bout, you crazy nigger?" queried James, still sitting in the boat, with dark salty estuary water all the way up to his waist.

"Ize laughing cause de water am only bout two feet deep! I put my toes down and dey dug into de mud."

The two men to slogged through the mud and drug both themselves and the boat to the shore. The water-filled, sodden boat weighed substantially more than it did before their attempted maiden voyage, but the water helped support it enough that they could drag it along.

They got back to the dry land and collapsed on the muddy bank, right at the water's edge. "What is we gwine do?" wailed James.

"No probbem," said Joseph. "We needs tuh leave dis old wood boat in de water tonight and tomorrow, and by tomorrow night, de wood be swole shut. Den it hold us all rite, and not leak no mo! I heared dat trick from an ole man at dat plantation dey selled me to, an he swears dat it works ebbry time."

James and Joseph attempted to make the boat's current position, half submerged near the bank, look as natural as possible as if the boat had drifted out with the tide and was in its final resting place. The men feasted on oysters that were in the mud alongside the bank, as they were exposed by low tide. The salty taste of the estuary water flavored the slimy shellfish enough that each of the two ate dozens. The food didn't help their overall attitude as both men grumbled and cursed the unwanted delay. They again swept clear their footprints, returned to their nest, and prepared to spend another long night and day fighting the blood-thirsty mosquitoes for limited sleeping space.

Finally, finally, finally, the interminable twenty-four hours passed, and nightfall began to descend and the shadows once again, began to deepen. The mosquito-bite covered, mud-caked men quietly and cautiously crept down to the shore, and lay in the dark shadows until they was sure that they detected no noises or motions.

They had come too far and been too lucky to this point to take unnecessary risks now.

Finally convinced that they were absolutely alone, they moved out into the shallows and began flipping the muddy water out of the boat with their hands. The boat gradually rose in the water, and floated much better than it had the night before. The constant inflow of water through the cracks had slowed perceptively to a few scattered trickles. They kept bailing until the boat contained almost no water at all. The would-be boatmen slithered carefully into the boat and shoved it out from the shore.

James and Joseph were nervous until they were convinced that the boat was going to stay completely on top of the dark water with them safely aboard.

After a few minutes, James laughed and nervously quavered, "Joseph, I reckon dat dis boat am gwine hold us up out ob de water. Dat ole man dat telled you bout dis trick helped us out, dat's fer shore. It dun saved us from startin a swim we cuddn't finish!"

Joseph responded, "Ize glad! Dis ole boat am ridin mitey high in de water, but we am still gwine need all de luck we kin git when we git closer tuh dose Secesh forts."

The men let the momentum of the boat and the sluggish river current carry them downstream. They removed the final remains of their tattered shirts from their backs and with great care, wrapped the oar locks in the cloth. It effectively muffled the noises.

Joseph cautioned James once again, "Eny noises from de time we git tuh dem lights round de bend an we be in deep trubble. We be slaves agin, mitey battered slaves and definitely not freemen. Iffen you feel like a sneeze iz coming, cubber you face in dat gunny sack, and hang on tuff. No noise! Enny noise, an we both be dead men!"

James responded with several vigorous, positive nods of his head and the two slowly moved toward the lights of the fort. They drifted whenever the sluggish current would allow and they paddled quietly when the ebb and flow of the river halted progress.

As the fugitives cautiously moved closer to the fort, they could faintly see the silhouettes of two Confederate soldiers, marching their sentry routes on top of the thick stone wall against the lights of the fort. Joseph made vigorous motions with his head, indicating the boat should be steered to the opposite side of the estuary, as far as away as possible from the fort and the soldiers. They moved so slowly that it felt like motion was not occurring at all.

Then they heard and felt a soft bump and the boat came to a complete stop. James and Joseph looked at each other in total consternation. Words were not possible or necessary, and they sat there for what had the appearance of an eternity. Pushing with the oars did absolutely no good and the boat remained firmly stuck on whatever had grabbed it.

After a long silence, James shrugged his shoulders, slipped out of his trousers, and slid gradually and carefully out of the boat. Keeping a death grip on the side of the boat, he did not relax until his bare feet dug into the soft, warm mud. As Joseph, seated in the stern, looked toward the bow of the boat in the darkness, all he could see of James was the whites of his eyes. He felt an insane urge to giggle but he wisely resisted the impulse.

James carefully reached down the bow of the boat and into the dark, murky water. He discovered that the boat had grounded on a mud bar. He pushed and strained, resolutely trying to move the boat backwards off the obstacle with muscle power. Simultaneously with a soft grunt from James, the boat slipped off the bar. James, startled by the lack of resistance, fell headlong into the foreboding water, making a soft splash. Joseph held his breath and remained perfectly still, as the boat drifted about ten feet backwards.

Joseph heard the sentries shout a challenge, then another. The two runaways could clearly hear the two soldiers discussing what the noise might have been for several moments, and Joseph heard the word "fish." Thankfully for the runaways, the sentries resumed their patrol. After taking the first breath in many moments, Joseph gave the boat a small push with a short stroke of the makeshift oar. He began to worry as he had not yet spotted James. The boat drifted slowly forward until James's hand appeared over the gunwale and gestured towards Joseph. Joseph finally figured out that James wanted the piece of rope that held up his pants. He untied it and passed it forward.

James secured the line to the front of the boat, then with great care used the rope to tow the boat behind him. He walked with all possible caution, slowly, quietly, and cautiously feeling for the muddy bottom with his toes before putting any weight down. After an eternity, the depth of the water dropped off and James was in deeper water to his shoulders. He slithered back into the boat, and the men began their journey once again. James carefully strained his eyes at the dark, murky water, trying to see any additional obstacles that might lie in or below the surface waiting to snag the boat and further impede their progress.

It was getting very late in the night and as they had successfully passed the fort, the two rowed into a small tributary and found a safe resting place for the next day. After the boat was tied off and the men retreated into the nearby woods, to James's amazement, Joseph suddenly began laughing. It was laughter that came from release of the unbelievable stress the two had been under.

"Ize you crazy," asked James?

"No, Ize not crazy, but you shore looks funny! Youse nekked as de day you wuz born and iffen yore face not black befo, it am now! I kin see nuttin but yore eyes and teeth," choked Joseph, still doubled up and panting with laughter. Tears ran down his cheeks, tracking through the day's accumulated dirt and grime.

James put a hand up to his face, and brought back a glob of sticky black mud. He wiped his face as best he could and, in spite of himself, joined Joseph in laughing. He also concluded that putting his trousers back on before the mosquitoes began their nightly feeding orgy was a prudent idea. The two men, having released some of their tension, were finally able to stop laughing. They lay back in the sand, feeling proud of themselves for having safely completed this most difficult part of their hazardous journey.

It took quite a while, but the men dropped off to sleep, all the while swatting at their usual bloodthirsty nighttime companions, the lowland mosquitoes. It seemed to be only moments since James had surrendered to sleep before he was rudely awakened by a sharp object poking into his side.

"Git up, boy," a gruff voice growled. "What is you doin here?"

Seventeen years of conditioning as a slave in South Carolina clicked into place in James's mind and he slipped quickly into his best slave-master tone of voice.

"I ain't doin nuttin, Massuh, Ize jes sleepin," said James in his Yassuh, Boss voice.

"I ain't yore Massuh, boy, nor is anyone else yore Massuh; you ain't no slave no more," answered the man, perhaps in a more kindly tone of voice.

James fully opened his eyes for the first time and to his amazement, he and Joseph were surrounded by eight soldiers, all in blue uniforms. Equally amazing, seven soldiers were black, like him!

"Whar is we?" queried James.

"You're on Sea Island, South Carolina, home of the First South Carolina Volunteers," responded the white officer. "What are you men looking for?"

"Thank Gawd! We wuz lookin for ya'll," blurted James, "But we didn know whar you wuz."

"Well, you found us," said the officer. "Let's go to our camp and maybe you can give us some information and we can see what you're up to. But first, we need to throw you in the pond over there so we can see what you two look like under all that South Carolina mud."

James and Joseph washed up, then followed the eight soldiers to a camp perched on the bank of the estuary. The camp consisted of new, tan canvas wall tents, numerous enough and sufficient in size to house a total of several hundred men. Horses and mules were tied up outside the camp. A pot of food was busily bubbling on the edge of a campfire, and the wonderful smell of the beef stew made the two mens' mouths water. James's belly growled loudly enough for the officer to hear. The officer threw back his head and laughed out loud.

"I guess your stomach is telling me that questions can wait for at least a little while. You men sit over here, and let's quieten that racket. Otherwise, we won't be able to hear each other talk! Private, get these men a plate full of that stew!"

James and Joseph sat on a log. One of the soldiers brought each of them a tin plate of stew with a warm piece of cornbread perched on top of the food. The stew was extremely hot, but that did not stop the two from diving in. The soldiers stood around and watched them gobble it down. The soldiers joked and guessed how long it had been since the new freemen had eaten. It took James and Joseph about two minutes to consume the stew and the black sergeant took the plates and promised them more after their stomachs had recovered from the shock of the first plateful of the hot, rich food.

"Now," started the white officer, "Let's find out what you two are up to. What exactly are you looking for, and how did you manage to find us?"

"Weze heard bout de Fus Souf round de plantation whar we libs for some time an we heared dat de Yanks was de officers fer de troops," began James.

"Dat's rite," chimed in Joseph. "Ebben after dey sold me up ribber, we still heared bout you. We thought meybe youins could use two more hard workin cullud men tuh fight de Secesh, so we started huntin whar you wuz."

"Well, you found us," said the officer. "If you can give the sergeant some facts about yourselves and who your owners were, we can always use good recruits. We're also interested in any information you might have about the location of any Confederate units or their dog patrols. Those damned patrols cost us a dozen recruits a day. We've been talking about what we can do about them, but we're not strong enough yet to do anything."

James and Joseph followed the sergeant to his tent where he asked lots of questions, some of which they could not honestly answer. However, James and Joseph gave him enough information about themselves and what they knew about their plantations and the Confederate presence in the area to satisfy him. He told them to sit and wait and he went over to talk to the white officer.

The officer walked to the tent and barked out an order to the two men, "Stand at attention." They stood and raised their right hands, following his instructions. He swore them into the Union Army and told them that they would receive nine U.S. dollars per month as privates. He also told them that their fighting had to be particularly ferocious. This was because the Confederates had issued orders that if members of a colored unit were captured, no prisoners would be taken of the soldiers and the white officers would be hung without a trial.

"Does this give you men any reason to regret signing up?" asked the officer?

"No," responded James, "Reckon we knowed dat it wouldn't be eny diffrunt from dat. Weze still reddy tuh fight!"

"All right, then, we have a few extra uniforms over there in the supply tent. Go over there and find one that fits. Pick up your shoes and a rifle from the other side of the wagon."

James and Joseph, moving as in a dream, followed the sergeant, and shortly exhibited a magical transformation into Yankee soldiers.

"Sergeant," groaned James, "How long do it take tuh git used tuh dese shoes on your feets? I ain't nebber had none like dese before. De las pair I had wuz made wid wooden soles."

The sergeant laughed, showing fine white teeth in his coal-black face. "Soon enuff, soon enuff. Dat last tent ober dere is you twos'. Go git settled in and we'll all eat dis time, stead ob jes watching you two dig in."

James and Joseph did as told and ate for the second time. This time they participated as full members of their new unit. These plates full of stew were eaten for the sheer enjoyment of eating, rather than from the necessity of quieting noisy growls of their bellies. The two ex-runaways, now soldiers, lurched to bed. They tossed and turned as their minds tried to absorb all of these events and their bellies tried to recover from the shock of good food. Eventually, sleep overcame them and the exhausted yet relieved James and Joseph slept, as the U.S. Army's newest and certainly greenest recruits.

CHAPTER NINE
THE WAR IN NORTHERN VIRGINIA
Nathan
Fall, 1862

The Holcombe Legion received its orders from the Army of Northern Virginia's Commander, General Robert E. Lee. In August, not too long after their absorption as a unit into the Confederate Army, the hustle and bustle and noises of substantial movement of men and equipment awakened Nathan with a start one morning before dawn.

He sleepily staggered from his small tent, stretched, and asked Luke, one of the nearest servants, "Whas goin on?"

The man replied, "We haz been given our orders--we leaves dis afternoon for North Virginia. Bes be gittin yore Massuh's gear together an yore's as well. The Yanks am a'waitin an we don wants to be late to de ball!"

Nathan rushed to Master Will's area, and found his master already dressed and giving orders to several sergeants.

"Nathan," began Will, "It's time for you to get our gear packed and ready to load. We're going to be traveling by train, so don't load up the horses with the packed gear. Keep it stacked in a pile and try to keep track of where it is—it'll be hard to find when we get to Virginia."

"Yassuh, Massuh Will, I'll git moving. Luke telled me that we don wants tuh be late to de ball. What'd he means?"

Will laughed. "He meant we're about to have our first full-blown confrontation with the Yankee Army. You'd best get started."

Nathan began by carefully packing Will's clothes and personal gear in the satchels and stacked them by the tent. He struck the tent, and rolled it up. Finished, he returned to his tent and repeated the operation there and carried his gear and his rolled up tent to stand by those of Will's. An hour later, the order to load came, and Nathan toted the equipment to the rail siding where the troop trains stood. Nathan's heart pounded as he looked up at the huge black steel monster, busily and loudly belching forth fire and black smoke from its stack.

He asked one of the servants standing close by, "Wha's it like, riding on dat ting? It look lik a monster a'sittin dar lik dat!"

The other man responded, "It ain't too bad--we ride on one comin ober here. We servants ride on dat open car ober dar, an de onliest ting you has tuh worry bout cides holdin on is watching fer sparks on you clothes. You kiver a lots mor ground a'ridin dat ting dan you does on foot or hossback!"

Not totally pacified, but less worried about this new adventure, Nathan helped load the mountain of gear and equipment. He carefully observed exactly where his and Master Will's gear went in the enclosed car, hopefully making it easier to retrieve once the Confederates reached their destination, wherever this Virginia was, anyway! He watched the horses as they were loaded on a number of cattle cars and soldiers were being herded onto their cars in the same way. Finally, he could delay no longer, so in spite of his fears and trepidation, he hopped aboard the open car along with the other body servants.

With a series of whistles and shudders, the train slowly pulled out of the station. With cheers of the local people ringing in his ears, Nathan moved out toward the next big adventure in his young life. He rode the first few miles with his hands over his ears. Once he got used to the constant belches, fits and starts and the click, click, click of the rails and cross ties, Nathan found that he could get used to train travel quite easily and he enjoyed the relative comfort.

The trip was made without incident, other than occasional delays caused by extremely heavy Confederate train traffic, mainly consisting of troops heading north. The few times the train was able to get up to full speed, Nathan found it breathtaking to watch the countryside rush by at an amazing thirty miles per hour. This was blinding speed indeed, for a young slave about to be away from his home state for the first time.

The train stopped several times during the day for replenishment of wood to fire the boilers and water to provide steam. On those occasions, the men were allowed to get off the train for a short time. Nathan found that leg stretching was, at the same time, both painful and a relief. The first order of business for all the men, officers and enlisted men, slave or free, black or white, was to rush to the edge of the nearest available woods to relieve painfully stretched bladders. Woe be unto he who suffered from soldier's revenge, or dysentery.

Food was sparse during the trip. It consisted mainly of cold corn cakes. Nathan was unable to locate Will in the mass of milling men, so he could only assume and hope that his master was able to find sustenance. Nathan watched in amazement as the topography of the countryside rushing by changed from the flat Coastal Plain of South Carolina to the rolling, forested hills of the western Carolinas and on into the Piedmont area of Virginia.

There the topography became even more marked, and the train struggled as it crept up the ever-steepening hills. Nathan hoped the train would successfully make it up all the hills, and would not have to be pushed by men, much like a wagon back home when it got stuck in the mud. He somehow felt that the train would be a truly unmovable object.

After a full day of managing only occasional restless catnaps, Nathan adjusted enough to the rocking motion of the train and the rhythmic click, click of the rails, that on the second day, he fell into a deep sleep. Fortunately for him during his sleep, the direction of the wind kept the blowing sparks from landing and burning holes in his clothes. These charred holes were the normally-seen badge of experience for those who rode on the flatcars pulled by the wood-burning steam locomotives of the times, but Nathan escaped this dubious honor.

After two extremely long days of traveling, the train ground to a halt. The mass of men was ordered off the train and was marched several miles up and down hill and cross-country. They were ordered to set up camp in a large, thick hardwood forest located near several cultivated fields. Nathan and the other servants began a frantic search for their Masters' gear. Nathan's earlier careful packing and location-spotting during loading of the train in South Carolina made it a fairly easy task to retrieve the equipment and he began setting up Will's tent. When he had almost completed setting up the camp, Will spotted him, and moved to Nathan's side.

"Don't bother making the camp very fancy, Nathan. I suspect that we'll be moving again very soon. The generals are trying to decide exactly when, where, and how we choose to meet the Yankees, and we'll have to move quickly."

Nathan asked, "Massuh, I bin a'tinkin. What do I do while de battle gwine on—whar do I go?"

"Will laughed and said, "Don't worry, Nathan, you'll be all right. The servants will be moved back behind the troops being held in reserve. If you're clever, you can find a hill with trees where you can climb up and watch the battle. Now, wish me luck—I've got to hurry."

"Yuh am de bes soldier in de Legion, an doze Yankees can't possbly hurt you," replied Nathan. "I'll sees yuh after de fight!"

"Thanks, Nathan," said Will, "Look for me after the battle."

Will moved off, shouting orders at his men. Nathan, saddened at the possibility of Will being harmed or worse, returned to the gear. Heeding Will's orders, he did not bother to set up his own tent, but kept it packed. A master sergeant came by the area where the servants were lounging in the clutter and ordered them to follow him. He led the slaves and servants to an area in the rear of the troops held in reserve. He told them to wait there for further orders.

Nathan remembered what Will had said, and looked around for a big tree. He followed the lead of several other servants and climbed as high in a massive oak tree as he could. From his perch, he had a good view of the beautiful rolling countryside of northern Virginia. He could see off in the distance, a creek which lazily flowed through the center of the green cultivated fields. He could also see nearby a large mass of men milling around, and recognized them by the gray uniforms as Confederate troops. As hard as he searched, he could not identify the men of the Holcombe Legion in the sea of gray. He watched the frantic proceedings with profound interest balanced with almost overwhelming fear. He was startled as he heard several tremendous booms which shook even the large tree in which he was perched.

Nathan's eyes followed where his ears indicated the sounds came from to a hill across the stream which divided the battlefield. Looking closely on the other side, he could see that the uniforms of the men firing the cannon were blue. He had his first look at real, live Yankees. He watched with horror as some of the shells the Yankees were lofting into the air struck the ground in the midst of the masses of Confederates and gray-clad bodies were tossed around in the air like so many leaves in the fall when they fell to the ground.

Then, as he watched further, the nearby Confederate cannon began answering the Yankee barrage, and he saw several Yankee cannon along with their crews of men disappear in a cloud of smoke split asunder by bolts of fire as ammunition blew up. He felt relief that the Confederate Army was going to give as good as it received.

Nathan remained up in the large oak tree most of the day, and watched the battle through the clouds of dust which made the earth look as if on fire. The waves of first blue, then gray uniforms, swept back and forth across the open fields, crossing and re-crossing the creek. Every time the cannon fired, Nathan cringed and his nerves jumped; it was likely that he could never get used to the earth-shattering roar and the resulting shake of the ground and the tree. The dust and smoke became thicker and thicker, making it almost impossible to see any detail of the panorama of battle going on before him.

Toward dusk, the blue uniforms retreated further across the creek and up the hills on the other side than either army had done during the day. The gray uniforms pursued them, screaming wildly. Nathan reasoned that the activities of the day were over and the gray-clad Confederates had been victorious. He stiffly climbed down from his perch. After rubbing his limbs and hopping around to restart his blood circulation, he hurried toward Will's tent, awaiting further orders and to be ready for whatever events were to happen next.

The closer Nathan got to the area where he hoped to spot his master, the more absolutely wild and chaotic the nightmare scene became. The thick red dust choked his every breath, and the milling soldiers and support personnel rushed hither and yon, creating a total madhouse. The cries, curses, prayers and screams of wounded men mingled with the shrieks of mortally-wounded horses. No one appeared to have any purpose in their running about. It reminded Nathan of chickens at home running around even after their heads had been chopped off.

Nathan became more and more concerned, as his search for Will continued to be unsuccessful. His worry was moving close to panic. Then he spotted a roan mare similar to the one which Will rode coming at a leisurely pace toward him. He rushed to the horse as he saw the rider was slumped over the saddle horn, holding on for dear life. He identified Will and he grabbed the reins of the terrified horse and led it to the tent area, after first stroking the horse and speaking to it in a low voice to calm it down. He eased Will off the horse and placed him ever-so-gently on the ground. Will's eyes were open, but he was barely coherent.

"Nathan, is that you?" he gasped out.

"Yassuh, Massuh, it am me. Ize worried bout you, but youse here. Whar is you hurt?"

"It's my arm--I took a Minie' ball in my upper arm and I've lost a lot of blood."

Nathan carefully cut away Will's upper uniform sleeve, to take inventory of the wound. There was indeed a lot of blood--it soaked Will's uniform and shirt all the way down to his fingertips. Nathan carefully prodded in the vicinity of the wound, but did not feel the bullet.

He said, "Massuh Will, I don't find de bullet, but mebbe we'd best git you tuh de surgeon and lets him look at it."

Will was too weak from loss of blood to argue, but he raised his good arm and grasped Nathan's upper arm. He looked Nathan squarely in the eye.

He sternly told him, "Nathan, I don't care what you have to do to prevent it, but don't let them take my arm! A one-armed man is no good as a soldier, much less as a planter."

Will passed out and slumped back. Nathan picked him up, and carried him toward the surgeon's tent. When the struggling slave toting his moaning burden arrived, Nathan once again gently lay Will on his back. He went to report his master's presence to the surgeon's helper.

Several hours later, Nathan was awakened from a cat nap at Will's side by the appearance of the surgeon. He wore a long white coat, stained reddish-brown with dried blood from top to bottom.

The man roughly brushed Nathan aside and took a cursory look at Will's arm.

"It's got to go, we've no time for working with it otherwise," brusquely stated the doctor. He turned on his heel prepared to rush off to more critically wounded men.

"But, Massuh, Massuh Will telled me tuh not let them takes his arm, fore he passed out," stammered Nathan.

"Shut up, boy," said the surgeon, "I've no time for argument with a damned slave. Move the hell out of my way. I can't stand here and argue about anything!"

He motioned for the nearby stretcher bearers to carry Will to the line formed in front of the tent where the worst screams and shrieks emanated. As he watched with horror, Nathan saw a detached leg with a boot still on, come flying out of the tent, and land on a stack of other limbs—the stack was easily as high as the top of Nathan's head.

Nathan stood stock still, and his head whirled with indecision, but Master Will's last coherent orders had been crystal clear. Nathan suddenly made up his mind, lunged past the stretcher bearers, and unsnapped Will's holster. He grasped the revolver, and pointed it at the doctor.

"Massuh Will told me tuh save hiz arm an I haz tuh do dat. Leaves him alone, an I'll tek ker ob him. If you ain't gots time fer him, I doz."

The surgeon stopped in his tracks, unable to speak. His face turned beet red and Nathan was deathly afraid of what was bound to follow.

"Boy, don't you know they will hang you if you use that revolver? You, a slave aren't supposed to even touch a firearm, much less threaten a white man with one. Now put that damn thing down before someone sees you!"

"I knows all dat, but I also knows what Massuh Will says tuh me. I haz tuh do what he say," quavered Nathan.

To Nathan's absolute amazement, the surgeon threw back his head and laughed. "I believe you really would use that gun on me. We can't have that, either for your sake or especially for mine. Let me take another look at your master's arm and I'll see if we'll be able to do anything."

The surgeon's more kindly tone convinced Nathan of his sincerity and Nathan reluctantly lowered his arm and let the revolver point toward the ground. His knees shook. The surgeon dropped to one knee by Will's stretcher and more slowly and carefully examined the wound. He prodded the area where the Minie' ball had gone in and, with Nathan's help, gently rolled Will over to his stomach. This time, he probed where it had exited Will's arm.

"The bullet passed through the arm and missed the bone, so that's not a problem. There's some muscle damage, but maybe we can save the arm. Boy, can you follow orders for me as well as you did for your master?"

"Yassuh, jes tells me what tuh do, and I kin do it," responded Nathan. "I needs to do what Massuh Will tells me to do—I be de bes body servant in the Federate Army."

The surgeon laughed once again. "Damn, boy, I reckon you're just that. You also made me laugh twice in the midst of this hell, and I thank you for that. Now hush a minute and let me give you instructions. I'm going to clean out the wound, treat it with sulfur powder, and dress it. You watch closely what I do, because you'll have to do the same every day until it heals because I don't have time. Watch carefully for red streaks down his arm, and if the wound begins to smell bad, get him over here immediately. We'll then have no choice but to take the arm. Now, help hold him down, because this cleaning is going to hurt, but it has to be done. We have to get the powder and any fragments of lead out of there or the arm will get infected for sure and all this will have been for nothing."

Nathan slowly and gingerly placed the revolver on the ground, did as he was told, and the surgeon probed and cleaned Will's wound. Nathan and one of the stretcher-bearers held the thrashing Will as still as they could. After treatment of the wound, Nathan enlisted the aid of one of the litter bearers to help carry the now unconscious Will back to his tent, where he was made as comfortable as possible under the circumstances.

During the night, Nathan moved his pallet onto the floor of Will's tent. Here, he would be able to immediately respond if his master needed any attention. Several times that night, Nathan was awakened by Will's loud and anguished groans, and Nathan immediately jumped up and tended to his needs. Will had a fever and was almost incoherent, but Nathan wetted a cloth and wiped his brow, giving him a small measure of relief.

Each time Will awakened it was harder for Nathan to fall asleep again. Once, Nathan lay back on his pallet, and looked around him at the interior of Will's wall tent. The glow of the campfire coals in front of the tent faintly lit the tent with an eerie orange glow. Will's gear, hurriedly stacked in every available corner of the tent, almost took on sinister shapes in the dim light. For a moment, Nathan felt a chilling fear, and sat upright on the pallet. When he stopped shaking, he forced himself to lie back down.

He lay there for a moment and thought of home. Even the old, rickety, weather-beaten shack back in the slave quarters in South Carolina looked wonderful in Nathan's musings. He imagined his Momma standing in the doorway, waiting to give him a big hug, and James and Stephen were behind her with big, welcoming grins on their faces. With these pleasant reveries of home drifting through his tired mind, Nathan languidly drifted back to sleep.

Nathan was awakened in the morning by Will's struggles to sit up. Nathan hurried to restrain the wounded man. Will croaked the urgent question that had apparently been on his mind all nigh through his half-sleep, half-coma. "My arm--have I still got it?"

"Yassuh, Massuh, it warn't easy, but you still has yore arm," hurriedly responded Nathan.

Will said, "Thank God for that. How long have I been unconscious, anyway?"

"Jes one night," said Nathan. "But you needs tuh rest--the doctor says so. Now, lie back down, an let me tek keer ob you. The word round camp is dat since we won, we don has to move fer a few days. Now rest!"

Will obeyed. Nathan's tone of voice gave him no choice. He went right back to sleep, this time more soundly, as snores soon filled the air. Nathan stayed near him for the remainder of the morning. Nathan managed to talk the mess sergeant into making some soup at lunch time. He carried the soup back to the tent and found Will awake and more alert.

"Here, Massuh Will, you needs food tuh get stronger. Kin you feed yourself, or do you needs me tuh hep you?"

Will responded by taking the spoon in his good hand and devouring the bowl of soup in no time. He relapsed again into a healing sleep, and Nathan did the same, napping for about an hour.

When Nathan arose from his nap and saw Will was still sleeping peacefully, he stretched like a big cat and stepped outside the tent to look around. He saw one of the body servants from the adjacent officer's tent walking in the direction of the battlefield of the day before, at Manassas Junction, Virginia. Nathan hailed him, "Hey Luke! Whar am you goin?"

Luke responded, "Ize gwine down tuh de battlefield, whar de Yankees cut an run. I hears dat dey lef lots ob good tings, and I aims tuh scrounge some."

Nathan pulled on his trousers, checked once more on Will and verified that he was sleeping soundly. He accompanied Luke down to the bloody field. The scavengers joined other servants and soldiers and found that lots of knapsacks had been tossed aside by Northern soldiers in the mad dash to escape the oncoming successful Confederate soldiers. They carefully avoided examining the bodies of the dead soldiers for shoes and other valuables, although Nathan saw other men doing that. Nathan filled a knapsack he found with food, clothes, razors, blankets, and several small cookpots. He found a gold watch lying on the ground He added that to the knapsack's contents. Nathan carried his spoils back to Will's tent, and found his master just coming to, from his hard afternoon nap.

Nathan showed Will his collected spoils of battle, and Will commended him for his cleverness. He refused to take the watch that Nathan offered, insisting that Nathan keep it. Will said it would make a good keepsake which Nathan could pass on to his children some day. Nathan added to the weight of his coat by sewing the watch into the cloth lining, alongside of the several gold pieces which he had already placed there from his sock-washing enterprise of the past several months.

Over the next few days, Nathan tended to Will's every need, and daily religiously cleaned the wound and changed the dressing. Fortunately, the rumors in camp were correct and the troops weren't moved for several days. Also to their relief, no ominous red streaks appeared, and no tell-tale odors signifying gangrene were observed. After the five day period of convalescence and careful tendering recommended by the surgeon, Nathan accompanied Will in the walk to the hospital tent. There the surgeon pronounced that Nathan's ministrations were successful.

"Lieutenant," said the doctor, "You owe a great deal of thanks to your servant. In my mindless rushing about following the conclusion of the battle, I was ready to perform the amputation of your arm, because I felt that I didn't have time for other treatment. Your man strongly convinced me otherwise."

Will looked at Nathan with a questioning glance. "How did he do that," Will queried. "What do you mean by strongly?"

"Actually, it was at gun point, with your handgun, but I admire rather than condemn him for his actions and his loyalty. He forced me to be a doctor, rather than a battlefield butcher, for a moment, and he truly showed his devotion to you. Because of his action, you still have a functioning arm on each side of your body!"

Will again looked at Nathan with a puzzled expression and thanked the physician again. The doctor hurried away to other duties. After a brief thoughtful period, Will said, "Nathan, I thank you. I was sure anyway, but this incident convinces me further that I made a wise decision when I selected you as my body servant. I'm also glad that no one else besides the doctor saw you with that gun—you might have been shot, no matter how good your intentions!"

"It warent nothin ," said Nathan. "I wuz jes doin whut you telled me tuh do. Dat doctor's eyes did git to be bout de siz of saucer plates when he saw dat gun in my hands an he wasn sure whether or not I wuz gwine use it. Iffen I had to, I reckon I would have!"

"Anyway, thanks," said Will. "Let's go to the command tent and find where our destiny lies, and where that part of the Holcombe Legion that wasn't destroyed is located, so we can join them."

They walked to the tent and found the Legion had been marched the day before to the small town of Manassas Junction. They were preparing to board another train, heading for the Maryland area and their next engagement. Will and Nathan hurriedly packed all of their gear on the horses and rode over to the Junction and the railroad station. There they were reunited with the rest of the Legion. Will told the story of Nathan's intervention over and over again, until Nathan became a unit hero. With somewhat less fanfare than had heralded their last train trip, the Legion loaded on the train, this time as experienced troops that had not only ridden trains before, but now had seen the elephant in battle, and survived.

Accompanied by belches of smoke and sparks and whistle-blowing, the train shuddered and the remnants of the weary and wounded Legion pulled out towards their next engagement, still full of hopeful optimism for the Confederate cause. During the train trip, frequently marked with stops to take on coal, water, or additional troops, Nathan joined the other body servants finding whatever food, clothing, and medicine they could locate in the surrounding countryside. The Legion had very few supplies of any kind and at the speed with which they were now traveling, they had far out-stripped any re-supply wagons that might be sent after them.

☐ ☐ ☐ ☐

CHAPTER TEN
BACK ON THE HOMEPLACE
Stephen
Winter, 1862

On the Low Country plantation, the slaves continued to work unsupervised. With the advent of winter, work in the fields had slowed down a little, although there was still plenty to do with the winter crops and in preparation of other fields. Stephen believed that life was still much better than it had been under the old overseer. The only regular grumbling among the field hands was that the supplies and special treats from the Big House, freely given before the war, had trickled to almost nothing.

Stephen, in his ever-increasing role as unofficial foreman and spokesman for the hands, listened carefully to the complaints. He took great pains to carefully consider Old Ned's stammering suggestions. Based on something Ned said, Stephen decided one evening to take a real chance. He discussed his plan with Momma and although she was a bit concerned about the white folks' reaction, she told him that he had to do what he felt best.

The next day, when Miss Annie and her girls brought the always appreciated lunch and water to the hands at noontime, Stephen waited for just the right moment. He approached her when no one else was near enough to hear their conversation.

"Miss Annie, kin I axe you someting?" Stephen blurted out.

"Of course, Stephen," replied Annie. "You know that I depend heavily on you for the crop work and I want to hear what you have to say. What is it?"

"Dar be some grumbling from de field hands and their families bout de fact dat dar be no good tings come down from de Big House since de war start. Iffin you could find someting tuh send down tuh de field hands on Sunday or sum nite, mebbe extra food or clothes, it make dem more happy and I spect dey will work better. I hopes you don't mind me axing dis."

Stephen finished his carefully rehearsed plea and took his first breath since he began. He waited both expectantly and fearfully for her response.

Miss Annie thought for a moment, and responded, "Stephen, you must know that there isn't as much food at the Big House as there was before the war, and we certainly haven't been able to buy any new clothes. However, I'll look around in the wardrobes to try and find some unused clothes to bring down. We'll also see if we can increase the food allotment, particularly for special occasions. Just make sure the other hands and their families know that we in the Big House aren't living as well as we were before the war, either, but we'll do the best we can under the circumstances. Thank you for bringing this to my attention. It's important that you hands are as comfortable as we can possibly make you--we're depending on you."

Stephen stammered, "Den you don't mind dat I axed yuh dis?"

"Not at all," said Miss Annie. "Please bring anything else that is on your mind to me, and I assure you that I'll respond, as best I can."

"Tanks, Miss Annie, I do dat." Stephen re-joined the other hands. He felt a mixture of relief as well as being rather proud of himself. If Miss Annie came through with goodies and the other hands found out it was Stephen who had approached her, he would be even more solidly rooted in his role as unofficial overseer and spokesman.

The next Saturday evening, true to her word, Miss Annie rode her favorite mare to the clearing where the slave cabins were located. Accompanying her was a wagon driven by one of the house slaves. The wagon contained several boxes.

As the slaves gathered around the wagon, Miss Annie stood up in her stirrups, and said, "Stephen tells me you're in need of additional clothes and food. The food supply is scarcer than it was prior to the war breaking out, but we've managed to obtain a few chickens and some vegetables. Maybe you'll be able to have a good meal tonight. We've also brought some unused clothes, including most of Master Richard's so you can feel a bit more festive when you attend church tomorrow." She looked at Stephen and said, "Thank you, Stephen for bringing this suggestion to me. I'm glad we were able to find a few treats."

She wheeled her dun mare in a tight circle, and rode back toward the Big House with cries of, "Tanks, Miss Annie," ringing in her ears.

Several of the field hands came by Stephen and slapped him on the back with thanks. During the chicken feast Momma fixed for dinner, she looked at Stephen with pride and wonder in her eyes.

"Stephen," she began, "Ize proud ob you. Axing Miss Annie for dose tings mus hab been hard. Youze really growin up, an your Poppa would hab been real proud ob you, today."

Stephen looked down in embarrassment, and passed off the deed with a foot shuffling in the dust and an "aw-shucks," but Momma continued to sing his praises the rest of the evening, not only to Stephen, but to anyone else who would listen. The next day, there were services at the small Episcopal chapel which the owner family had built some years before for themselves and the slaves' worship. Stephen thought that the singing had never been so beautiful, and the girl from the next-door cabin had never looked so pretty. He attempted to talk to her after church. He approached her, but his courage deserted him and he fled in a near-panic.

Life went back to normal the next day, and the field hands began preparations for next spring's cotton planting, necessary to the life of the plantation, as well as to the survival of the Confederacy. It did seem, however, that this year was different. It was more satisfying to the field hands who had supervised themselves in planting, hoeing, and harvesting. Stephen noticed the hands would occasionally even sing, when several men found themselves near the end of their respective rows at the same time. There had not been much singing to now, and the spirituals lifted the spirits of all the hands. Stephen felt pride and he strove to continue to prove the responsibility that Miss Annie had placed on him as "ad-hoc" overseer. He was proud, but still not quite sure enough of himself to talk to that pretty girl. It would take additional shots of self-confidence before he would be ready for that, but it would come sooner or later, it would come!

The word came down through the slave grapevine that Master Will had been slightly wounded in a battle in northern Virginia. Happily, it wasn't enough to really slow him down or even to win him a trip home for convalescence or furlough. Stephen found he was concerned about Master Will's well-being, and was glad to hear about the relative insignificance of the wound.

CHAPTER ELEVEN
AND THE MARCHING WENT ON, AND ON, AND ON
James
Winter, 1862

On one of the Sea Islands, James and Joseph were beginning to wonder if all one ever did in the Yankee Army was march. The First South held drills twice a day for several hours. On days when new recruits signed up, they drilled a third time to catch the new men up. James and Joseph had a great deal of trouble with their feet, as 19 or 20 years of barefoot living had caused their feet to spread. Their now-shod feet protested loudly at being crammed into stiff, new brogans. Eventually, the shoes broke in and feet toughened along with the rest of their bodies, and they found themselves in excellent physical condition. James also admitted to himself after weeks of this, that the soldiers as a drill unit looked pretty dadgummed good.

He overheard the white officer say one day to a visiting officer, "These coloreds are actually as good or even better than our usual recruits, particularly at marching and drill. They seem to enjoy the military life. Now if they only prove to be as good at fighting as they are at marching and drilling."

James thought to himself, just watch us--not only are we fighting for our freedom, but we're fighting for our lives every battle. We'll be the best fighters you've ever seen, of whatever color! Just hide and watch!

Three days later, it appeared than James was going to get a chance to either prove or eat his words. Right after breakfast, the Captain lined up the troop, and announced, "Men, get your gear together--we leave in an hour for an excursion up the PeeDee River. It takes lots of material to supply an army, even a small one like ours. We're looking for lumber and to collect a little livestock and maybe make life tough on a couple of plantations and the owners. We'll free whatever slaves are left on those plantations, and maybe pick ourselves up a few more recruits. If there is any cotton picked and ready for shipping, we'll burn it. Then, we'll return here, where the Secessionists are afraid of our strength. Now, go get ready to prove yourselves for the first time as full members of the Union Army. We leave within the hour."

James and Joseph hurried to their tent and rolled their gear up in blankets and tied them across their knapsacks. They had been ordered to do this in the event the visit upriver turned into an all-nighter. They strapped the bedrolls on their backs. James and Joseph checked and rechecked their rifles, and hung ammunition pouches from their belts. The two men stood outside of their tent, ready and eager to go. It seemed forever before the captain called for the troops to form their lines.

The entire troop was standing at attention in perfect parade ground files, and the captain nodded at the sergeant. He gave the command to move out, and the First South Carolina Volunteers started their first mission, into an enemy-filled countryside. As their base was located in the heart of South Carolina's coastal plain country, every move they made was certainly reported ahead to people in their path. They could be sure of resistance from unseen sources as they marched.

The troops moved in the open at a steady pace and James and Joseph mentally compared this bold march across the countryside with the furtive way in which they, as runaways, had crossed much of the same ground they covered just a few weeks ago. To everyone's surprise, no shots were fired at them. The relative strength of the First South was more than local resistance troops could muster, so no contacts were made.

The troop marched for about half of the day before the scouts spotted the first plantation. The advance guard boldly proceeded to the door of the Big House, and the captain gave orders to search the place and secure it. The troops moved as veterans and discovered that the white residents were gone. One of the First South came from the woods, pushing several ragged slaves in front of him.

"Whar am yore Massuhs?" asked the sergeant.

"Dey run several days ago--dey wuz afraid ob us slaves an ob you sojers," stammered one of the slaves. "What am you gwine do wid us?"

"We ain't gwine do nuttin wid you, cept set you free. You ain't got no Massuh anymore," proclaimed the sergeant. "You can come back wid us tuh Sea Islands and jine up as soldiers, or stay here. But, I warn you, we don't intend tuh leave much standing at this here place."

The sergeant began shouting orders and the troops spread out to comb the property. The soldiers spent most of the rest of the day tearing out the best lumber that could be found and the wagons were soon loaded to their groaning capacity. Some of the privates found several cows and a flock of chickens and ducks. They put the fowl in nets and slung them on the wagons and tied the cows to the tailgates.

When all was loaded, the sergeant ordered several privates to the warehouse, located next to the river. They lit torches, and tossed them into the warehouse onto the piles of cotton bales. Other soldiers set fire to the Big House. The black smoke billowed up. As the day was waning and the afternoon shadows were lengthening, the captain ordered the troops to move out.

"That smoke will bring every Confederate in the area. We'd best move rapidly, back to our safe camp where they're afraid to follow us. We'll be back to visit more plantations until all the Secesh in this area get smart and leave."

The First South force-marched through the dusk and into the dark night. The weary soldiers finally arrived back at their camp. Unfortunately, they found that, in their absence, the camp had been almost completely trashed. Knife cuts were made on all the tents, the food had been stolen, and the fences the soldiers had so laboriously built to corral the horses and mules were scattered across the countryside. The high spirits of the soldiers after their successful raid were immediately dashed, as if they had received a bucket of cold water over their heads. The sergeant, after taking in the awful scene of destruction, began barking orders, and the weary soldiers dropped their knapsacks and bedding rolls and began setting things straight, as best they could.

The sergeant came over to James, and said in a low voice, "James, take one oder man and begin searching ober on de river whar de sentry post was and look for Private Washington. I haven't seen him, and Ize fraid he may not have made it."

James and another man lit torches and moved out into the dark towards the river bank and began searching. It took only a few moments to find the huddled body of the missing man. James and his companion found he had been literally beaten to death. The two men sadly carried the bloodied and battered body back to camp.

The sergeant called the soldiers over to view the body, and told them, "Dis here is what will happen tuh you iffen you forget for one minute bout what de Secesh has said bout us cullud soldiers. De local buckras dun did dis, soon as dey heard us move out dis mornin. Weze fightin tuh stop dis kind ob ting. Now, git back tuh work; sooner we finish, sooner we kin go tuh bed."

The soldiers complied with the sergeant's orders and returned the camp to a semblance of what it had looked like before, finishing at about three o'clock in the morning. The sergeant set out double guards, placing sentries on both the river side and the land side of the camp. Those lucky enough to not serve first watch immediately crawled into their tents and slept. Those who slept during the first watch felt as if they had been asleep for only five minutes when they were shaken awake to serve their watch. The memory of the body of Private Washington had made an impression on all of them, and, for a change, no one complained about serving watch duty, even in the night when all the trees and bushes took on sinister shapes in the dim glow of the campfire coals.

Life in the camp went on as before, with lots of drilling and marching, and the men settled into the routine. Days stretched into weeks and weeks into months. The First South made two additional successful raids on plantations up-river and they added to their muster rolls each visit by signing additional recruits. The First South was shaping up as an effective, fully-staffed fighting unit. The regiment had a full complement of five hundred trained, armed, and equipped fighting men.

James and Joseph talked many times about the roll of the dice that led to their current situation. They believed they had been lucky in choosing the route to the South Carolina Sea Islands. The men felt they were doing at least a small part in helping themselves and their people gain and, maybe even more importantly, earn their own freedom. The harassing tactics that the First South was performing in the surrounding countryside was playing havoc with the lives of the people of the plantations in the Coastal Plain territory and the men of the First South were proud of that accomplishment.

CHAPTER TWELVE
THE MARYLAND CAMPAIGN
Nathan
Winter, 1862

After another back-breaking train ride, the Legion found itself in the vicinity of South Baltimore, Maryland. The responses from local people in the border state were mixed. Some showed signs of welcoming them with open arms, others looked at them as if they hoped the invaders would disappear off the face of the earth. The confused border state status of the State of Maryland showed all the way down to individual citizens. Nathan rode beside his master and took in all the new sights with wide open eyes. He saw envying looks cast his way by some of the few Negroes he spotted along the way. He rode just a little straighter and taller and he felt just a bit prouder. The Legion set up a quick camp for the night, west of Baltimore.

Will told Nathan that the officers of the Legion expected to face the Yankees once again either tomorrow or the next day.

Nathan nodded, and told Will, "Massuh, I reckon dey be proud dat dey wounded you onct, but dem Yankees not git lucky again. We worked too hard tuh fix you up. You be kerful tomorrow--no Minie' balls!"

Will laughed. He walked down the row of tents, checking on his men. Most of them were still extremely tired and sick, after the hard campaign at Manassas Junction, followed by the long train ride. Nathan watched him go and sat on a log and reflected. It certainly had been different since Master Will had been wounded and Nathan had carried out his order to save his arm. It was almost as if the black man and white man were friends, not master and slave. This was an unheard-of relationship in the 1860's. Will was now telling him about future plans of the Legion, and what the officers planned to do next. Nathan liked the current situation and he vowed to continue doing whatever he could to assure that it would not change back to the way things once were.

Night came and the Legion slept. Nathan lay on his bedroll in his tent and listened to the muffled snores and the sounds of the sentries as they softly called back and forth from post to post, with "all's wells." It felt like he had been soldiering his entire short life, not only a few long months. He was mighty worried in the long run about what would happen because of the war, but as he slipped off to sleep, he felt completely content for the time being.

Morning came and with it, the breaking down of camp and the now-familiar loading of gear onto the horses and into the Legion's mule-pulled wagons. Nathan felt comfortable with the routine. He was one of the first servants perched up on his horse beside his master, ready to move out. Finally, move out they did, heading west. As the day wore on, Nathan could see faintly in the distance, blue-gray shapes which reached up to touch the skies. It was sure that he had never seen anything like them in the flatlands of South Carolina, or even in the hilly Piedmont of Virginia!

"Massuh," Nathan asked, "What be dose big tings I sees way ober dar?"

Will responded, "Those are mountains; the biggest one is

called South Mountain. I understand we're heading right for it. The coming battle with the Yankees may be near, or even on, that mountain."

Nathan kept his many other questions to himself. He became more and more interested in the mountains, as the now-seasoned fighting unit moved closer. The mountain became larger and larger and less and less a subdued hue of blue. Shapes became evident and gradually clarified into details of steeply-sloping rocks and trees.

The Legion stopped for the night a few miles from the mountains and Nathan found it difficult to keep his mind on his work. His attention was on the monstrous shapes looming out of the dusk. He knew he had never seen anything so beautiful, and the red, purple, and pink colors of the sunset to the west were truly breath-taking. At the same time, the mountains cast a sense of foreboding on these soldiers who had the effrontery to camp on their steep slopes, much less to try and march up the slope, dragging horses, supplies, and even cannon up the mountain. Fight a battle on the slopes of such a mountain? Sheer arrogance to think such a thought, much less try to carry it out.

The next day as the caravan drew nearer, Nathan could see, off in the distance, a road which went straight up the steep mountain. As he could have guessed, that is where the Legion headed. The dusty, exhausted unit stopped more frequently than usual to let the horses, mules, and men take breathing spells. It took most of the day to gain the crest of the slope. The Legion spread out across the ridge, and the soldiers began digging in, as best they could on the rocky slopes. They were able to prepare relatively secure breastworks with a combination of naturally-occurring rock outcrops and filling in between huge rocks with dirt and smaller rocks. A direct attack of Yankees on this line might succeed if enough numbers attack, but many of those attackers would be lying dead on those slopes by the end of the fight and those men would certainly no longer care about the game of "king on the mountain."

Nathan commented to Will, "Do you reckon dat dose Yankees be crazy enuf tuh come up dat hill wid us on top? Dere's no way I would try dat."

Will answered, "Those bluebellies certainly are crazy enough, or maybe brave enough. From what I understand, there are lots more of them than there are of us. Maybe being on top will help equalize the numbers. We have to stop them here, or at least slow them up substantially, or the Yanks will cause havoc on the other side of South Mountain over the next few days and weeks."

Will said, "Now, let's get some sleep--I think tomorrow is going to be a long, hard day, and I'm afraid that we might lose quite a few of the troops we have left. That battle at Manassas really decimated our ranks. The Legion is at less than half-strength. Some of the other regiments in the brigade at Manassas were fortunate and didn't see much action—we're counting on them to carry the brunt of the fight here, cause we're surely not able."

Nathan crawled into his tent, wrapped himself in his blanket, and reflected on what Will had said. Nathan didn't believe for one minute that Will had any fear in him, but he definitely sounded worried. With those thoughts chasing around in his head, he drifted off to sleep.

It felt like only a few minutes later; it was definitely still pitch-dark, when Nathan was awakened by the familiar noisy sounds of a rising army. He heard axes ringing cutting firewood, and sergeants yelling at sleepy, still-exhausted soldiers, trying to get them moving. He drug himself out of his warm blanket, stretched, started a small fire, and fixed Master Will's breakfast. The coffee he brewed in the past had never tasted as good as it did up on that mountain, on top of the world.

Before Nathan could clean the dishes, Will told him, "Run along up that way where the supply wagons are parked, just on the other side of the ridge. It should be safe there, and you'll be out of harms way during the battle."

Nathan dropped the still-dirty pot he was holding, and hastily departed in the direction Will was pointing. He found the other servants, located on the opposite side of the reserve troops. He hunted a tree to climb, much as he had done at Manassas. Being on the opposite side of the ridge, it was more difficult here, and he was unsuccessful in finding a satisfactory perch to watch the battle.

Nathan could hear the sounds of the fighting, as the cannon began their deafening roar; the Legion's cannon were louder because they were closer. He heard the Southern yell as it echoed across the mountains from peak to peak. He could also hear the Yankees' responding shouts, and the feared blue uniformed troops were coming closer, judging from the sounds of battle. He occasionally heard the shrill noise a bullet made as it passed near his location. Several times he heard the scream of an incoming shell that had been shot too high for its intended target and crashed on the back slope of the mountain behind him.

Nathan heard one of the body servants on the ground exclaim, "Whoo, listen tuh dat noisy tail! Look out, all ob you t'ree thousand dollah niggers--better come down outn dem trees!"

The sounds of the too-near bullets scared Nathan, but his curiosity was strong. He stayed up in the tree, watching as intently as he could to see how the battle was progressing.

The battle swung back and forth during the day, judging from the noises. Dusk approached. Nathan was suddenly startled to see hundreds, indeed thousands of Confederate soldiers running under his tree past him, and down the opposite side of the ridge.

Nathan looked around, and to his great surprise, he was alone! He had been so absorbed in listening and trying to interpret what was happening in the battle, that he hadn't noticed the other servants had come down and moved somewhere else. He almost panicked as he climbed down from the small tree which he had climbed to gain a little sight advantage. As he swung down from the last branch, he fell smack into the arms of a bearded burly white man, dressed in a blue uniform!

"What have we here," growled the man. "A small, colored Reb? What you doing up in that tree, boy?"

"Nothin, Massuh, Ize jes tryin to see what was goin on, dat's all," whispered Nathan. "Sides, I'm jes a body servant, not a Reb."

"Well, boy, what's been going on is that we just whipped your Masters' butts up here on this mountain. They've all run down the other side and left us in control. I reckon you is a free man now, not a slave. You've been captured by the army of the U.S. of America. Now, you going to give me trouble, or are you going to be good and do what I tell you while we decide what to do with you?"

"I'll be good," responded Nathan. "But, Ize worried bout Massuh Will, and what he a-tink iffen I not dere tuh fix his supper."

"Not your problem any more. You ain't got no master now," answered the big sergeant. "Now, get over there and sit on that log, while we figure what to do with you."

Nathan did as he was told and sat on the log for what felt like hours. A grumbling private brought him a tin plate loaded with hot food. Nathan, who was famished, hurriedly gobbled it down.

"Damn, boy, them Rebs never feed you?" asked the soldier.

"Yassah, dey feeds me, it's jes been all day since I et anyting an I wuz powerful hongry," answered Nathan.

The soldier brought Nathan a blanket, and motioned him to lie down and sleep in a small wall tent set up near the log where he was sitting. Nathan again did as he was told, but tired as he was, he lay there with wide open eyes, unable to fall asleep. All he could do was to ponder about what Master Will was going to think. Would he believe Nathan had run away? Nathan had promised to be as good a body servant as he could be, and sleeping here amongst the Yankees was certainly not being that. He also thought about how Will was becoming almost a friend, rather than just a Master.

After several hours, Nathan was still unable to go to sleep. He kept looking out the front flaps of the tent, situated such that all he could see was the campfire and the tents, set up in a circle, facing inward. The sounds of the Yankee camp slowly faded. Soon the only noise was the snap and pop of the coals of the campfires and the snoring of hundreds of men. That symphony of snoring was, at least familiar to Nathan and sounded no different from the noises in the Confederate camps.

After lying there sleepless for hours, Nathan made up his mind. He had to get back to Master Will, somehow. He had a problem because of the way the tent was situated. He could see nothing behind him. He quietly and carefully reached into his pocket and removed the jackknife which the Yankees had neglected to confiscate. He rolled over to reach the back of the small tent, and almost stitch by stitch, began cutting a hole in the tent, to serve both as observation port and escape route.

After Nathan cut the back of the tent out, he looked around him in the darkness. All he could see in the moonlight was the shape of the top of the ridge, looming above the sleeping men. He could hear but could not see the sentries walking their rounds. Then he identified a faint form who was walking in the direction Nathan needed to go to try and find Will. He concentrated until he established a pattern in the sentry's walking. When the sentry walked to the left, it took him about ten minutes before he returned. During that ten minutes, he was behind an outcropping of rock and out of earshot for a couple of minutes and could neither hear nor see the camp.

Nathan carefully timed his flight. He rose an inch at a time and stuffed a couple of branches into his blanket, plumping it up. He slithered out the cut in the back of the tent; the next time the sentry walked to the left, Nathan crept into the woods and up the hill,.

Nathan initially crawled approximately fifty feet into the darkness and hid behind two large trees. He waited until the sentry turned once more, only ten feet from Nathan's hiding place. The sentry walked behind the rocks. Nathan's heart was pounding so hard he was afraid that the sentry could hear it, but somehow he didn't. Then Nathan ran so hard up the steep slope, that he thought his heart was going to bust out of his chest. When he finally felt safe, he fell into a pile of leaves at the base of a big oak tree, and gasped for breath. When he could again draw a deep breath, he sat up and thought about his precarious situation.

Nathan reckoned that he, one small black body servant from the Low Country of South Carolina, was right smack dab between two very large armies of white men. What happened to him would be of small consequence to anyone but himself, if the blue and gray began fighting again on the morrow. He definitely did not feel good about his possibilities for longevity at that moment.

Nathan figured that he had better do something, as he had not improved his situation by his flight. He got up, brushed off the leaves, and slowly and cautiously began making his way down the back side of the mountain. In the distance, down the slope, he could see the dim glows of several campfires, hopefully Confederate. He made his way toward them, listening carefully for sentries.

When he heard, then saw a sentry to his right in the moonlight, he dropped to the ground behind a log. With quavering voice, he softly called out, "Massuh, please don shoot. Ize not de enemy."

"Who's there," shouted the sentry. "What's the password?"

"I don knows no passwords. Ize jes tryin tuh find de Federate Holcombe Legion an Massuh Will, dat's all," responded Nathan.

"Come into the light so I can see you," said the sentry. "Do it, right now!"

"Ize you gwine shoot me?" called Nathan.

"No, no, now come on out where I can see you! This is my last warning!"

Nathan slowly got up and walked into the light of the campfire, with his arms high in the air.

"I reckon you don't look too dangerous," laughed the sentry. "They tell me that the Holcombe Legion is the next unit, over there," and he pointed to the left. He kicked a sleeping soldier at his feet, and told the grumbling private, "Take this nigger over tuh the Holcombe Legion fore one of us sentries has tuh waste a perfectly good bullet on his worthless hide."

The soldier, mumbling and grumbling all the way about being rousted from his sleep, led Nathan through the woods. The two met up with the Holcombe Legion sentry on that side, and the private passed Nathan on to the sentry.

The sentry pushed Nathan into the dim light of the campfire, and called out, "If there's a Will who has lost a no-count slave, here he is."

The word spread through the camp, and Will walked up to the fire. He saw Nathan standing there, and after he was able to close his gaping jaw, snapped at the sentry, "That is certainly not a no-count slave! That's my body servant Nathan, and as of this moment, he is a free man! Nathan, what in the world happened to you? I've been looking all over and I was afraid you had fallen off the edge of the mountain."

Nathan listened carefully to the exchange, and it was time for his jaw to gape open. "Massuh, I wuz captured by de Yankees, an dey sayed dat dey wuz gwine tuh keeps me, but I tells dem dat I haz tuh tek keer ob you, and I told you dat I wuz going tuh be a good body servant, an, an . . ."

"Slow down, Nathan, slow down," laughed Will. "I can hardly understand a word you're saying. What happened next?"

By this time, virtually the entire camp had gathered around to hear the tale. Nathan continued, "Afer dey feeds me an tells me tuh gwine tuh sleep, I tooks my knive dat I picked up after de fus battle an I cuts a hole in de back ob de tent, den I lay dere an watched de sentry till I knowed what he wuz gwine do next, den I cuts and runs. I haz to hide on de edge ob dey camp till dere are no guards enywhar. I climbs ober de mountain, bumps into lots ob trees and rocks an almos falls into a big hole, den next ting I knows, I finds de Legion. I feels lik Ize home, dat's what!"

The listening men laughed and applauded the story. Several of the white soldiers came by to welcome Nathan back. One man told Nathan, "I wish all of our soldiers were as dedicated as you. And to make it even more special, you didn't even have to come back. The war could have been over for you. But, here you are."

Nathan and Will returned to the location where Will had set up his own tent for the night. Nathan looked at it with a critical eye.

"Looks purty good, Massuh Will, but I believes dat I kin puts it up straighter an more level!"

Will laughed, and said, "I'll give you the chance to put it up wherever we are tomorrow. Now, there's your blanket roll. Stretch it out by that tree, and let's get some sleep. Your Yankee friends will be on the move again, tomorrow, and we may have to meet them again."

As Nathan walked to where he would sleep, he told Will, "Massuh Will, dey ain't no friends ob mine--whar in de world did yuh git dat idea? Ize jes powerful glad I ain't wid dem no more."

Will laughed, "Just teasing you; go on to sleep."

The excitement abated, the camp resumed its sleep, and as excited as Nathan was, he had no problem whatsoever in joining them.

The next morning, Nathan awoke early, kicked the coals in the campfire, added fresh wood, and started the coffee. When Will joined him at the fire, Nathan asked Will, "Did you means what you said las night bout me bein free?"

Will responded, "Of course I did! I'll write the papers up today or as soon as I am able to get to the company clerk. I'll send a letter to Mother so she'll know what I've done. She'll have no problem with it, that's for sure. From this time on, you are a freeman, and you are working for me as my body servant. How about nine dollars a month as pay? I think that amount is what the Confederate government pays foot soldiers now, and you definitely help me to do more as a soldier. If you want, I'll hold the money for you as we go, and you should have quite a nest egg when the war is over. Is that all right with you?"

Nathan was practically speechless, but he managed to vigorously nod his head and he stammered out, "Thanks, Massuh, dat will be fine."

"Nathan," replied Will, "You don't need to call me Massuh any more. How about just plain Will?"

Nathan recoiled as if struck by a slap to the face. "But Massuh, dere's no way I kin do dat!"

Will laughed. "All right. Maybe that's moving a little too fast. How about Mister Will. Do you think your tongue can say that?"

"I reckon," responded Nathan, "I reckon I kin do dat."

The two settled down and made and prepared breakfast. Shortly afterward, the order came down to prepare to move out, so Will went back to Lieutenanting and Nathan went back to packing. Once again, the Holcombe Legion was on the move. Luckily, the unit was not to engage the enemy that day, although as they were moving off, they could hear the sounds of a major battle off in the distance, west of South Mountain. The weary members of the decimated Holcombe Legion did not mind in the least not being invited to that ball!

The Holcombe Legion marched 30 miles to the southeast, where the exhausted, dirty, and bloodied unit set up camp. They were happily able to spend about a week licking their wounds from the last two battles. The Legion had been greatly reduced in strength of numbers and supplies by Manassas and South Mountain. They had lost more than half of their enlisted men through death, wounds or capture, and the officers had to do a good bit of re-organizing to combine units back up to fighting strength. The time allowed the sick to recover, the supply wagons to catch up, and the slightly wounded to get back on their feet. A few replacement troops from South Carolina were rumored to be headed their way and would join them soon.

The remainder of the fall as winter rapidly approached was fairly easy for the Legion. They continued moving southeast, and had a few minor skirmishes against the Yankees. Neither force was eager to engage the other in a major battle, so the two armies parried and thrust but never squared off. The threatenings of winter found the Legion in northern Virginia.

Nathan rose one chilly morning, and sought out Will. "Mister Will, does you reckon dat we am in our wintering place? Iffn we is, Ize gwine tuh search out some supplies tuh make de tents more comfortable fore it get plumb cold."

Will responded, "I suspect that we are going to winter here, but you know the army. That's fine if you go ahead and get set for winter, but don't get unhappy if we have to move again."

Nathan began searching the countryside. Within a few days, he had installed wooden floors in both tents and built small tables out of packing crates. These would serve as a writing table for Will and a storage place for Nathan in his tent. With the help of several other servants, Nathan built a large magnificent fireplace sporting a stone back which directed heat in at least the general direction of the tents. Luckily after all his labors, the Legion was apparently going to winter there, and the work was not for naught. Nathan also gathered a large pile of cut wood, ready for burning. He noticed that around him, other servants and privates in the army had done the same.

When Will came back to his tent that night, Nathan told him, "Mister Will, I looked round here today, an deres not a stick ob wood for a mile! All of de fences and de barns bin tore down. Ize glad you telled me early dat it looked like we wuz going tuh stay here. It sho made it easier tuh git wood and such, so it did!"

"You've done a good job, Nathan," said Will. It will be a little more comfortable since you've protected us from the worst of winter's cold blasts."

Nathan also decided that the time had come to vary their diet, so he and his friend Luke did some scouting in the area around the winter camp. They found two small farms located a couple of miles or so to the east, one of which didn't look to be occupied. He and Luke got up before dawn one morning, and, having told their officers the evening before that they were going scouting, set out over hill and dale toward the farms.

The deserted farm was closer, so they wandered around its outbuildings. They did not find much of any interest around the buildings, so they went into the abandoned farm house. Again, there was not much that intrigued them as they went from room to room. Nathan found a closed door off the kitchen and he carefully opened the door to see what might be hidden inside. He immediately received a start, much like during his encounter with Brer Fox in the chicken coop some months before. He was face to face with a very startled, very large, and very angry raccoon.

Nathan jumped back, and called for Luke in a choked voice. "Luke, lookie here! I don knows who skairt who de mos!"

Luke walked to Nathan's side, and they watched as the Poppa raccoon who startled Nathan, Momma raccoon, and four small raccoons walk through a hole they had gnawed in a board near the floor, with as much dignity as they could muster. Nathan's heart slowed down to its normal pace and the two continued their search.

It was near the largest and most remote outbuilding, that they found their treasure. At least, this was where they first heard the treasure! The two heard a pig snort; they raced into the woods behind the building. They found a large pig, just the right size for a feast. The three of them, two determined men and one startled pig, wrestled in the fallen leaves for several minutes, until Nathan and Luke got him under control. It took them the better part of an hour to retrace their steps to the winter camp. They knew exactly where they wanted to go, but the pig had other ideas: he had absolutely no intentions of cooperating. When the three arrived in camp, Mister Will and Luke's master welcomed them and their dinner guest.

After the soldiers became convinced that there was not a farmer with a gun closely following the servants, and that they had indeed found the pig on an abandoned farm, Nathan and Luke were turned loose to prepare the meal. And, quite a feast it was! The four men sat around the campfire after numerous helpings of roast pig, and the conversation for a while consisted of mostly groans and belches. The groans were groans of contentment, to be sure!

The Legion settled into winter camp routine and they suffered only infrequent drills designed to keep the men alert. Will and the other officers spent time inspecting arms and making sure that men and equipment were ready for the spring campaigns. Nathan put his skills as "supply sergeant" to work and had Will set up in fine style.

Nathan also pitched in and helped a number of other servants and some of the enlisted men build a small chapel, in which the Legion chaplain would celebrate church services as the winter wore on. The chapel was barely large enough for fifteen men to enter, one at a time, but the rough-sawn boards that were used for the siding cast a certain rustic air about the place. The chaplain helped the men build a small rock and log altar, and he breathed a sigh of satisfaction as he stood side by side with Nathan to make a final inspection of the chapel.

The chaplain remarked, "It certainly will be a real pleasure holding services in this building--It is truly the House of God and I appreciate you mens' efforts. I especially thank you, Nathan, for leading the effort. The result is that, this fine structure is as holy as any Cathedral ever built by men."

The number of body servants remaining in the Legion had dwindled considerably since the war began, as a few had run away when the opportunity had presented itself. Many had been sent back home to help with crops and foodstuffs for the armies. This was necessary to replace the swelling number of runaways the plantations were experiencing, particularly on those plantations located near the war activities. As soon as the Yankee "saviors" came within a county or so of a plantation, many slaves took that as a good time to jump and run, and they did so. They were not exactly welcomed by the Union troops and officers, but the contrabands tagged along behind the Union troops and followed them as they moved around the countryside. Feeding and caring for this large number of camp followers provided the Northern armies logistical problems that they had to deal with.

These situations did not impact Nathan very much, except that he found his socks for five cents washing business increased daily with the lesser number of servants in the Legion. As he had done daily since he started his business, as soon as he completed his chores, he put the socks on to boil. Nathan then was able to find free time almost every day.

Fall was coming, and the color of the changing leaves made the surrounding hills spectacular to view. Fall in the hills of Virginia was much prettier than South Carolina Low Country, where seasonal changes were hardly noticeable. Nathan was amazed at the variety of oranges, reds, and yellows that appeared in a new kaleidoscope each day. Nathan, several times each day found himself just sitting on a log looking off into the hills, daydreaming.

☐ ☐ ☐ ☐

CHAPTER THIRTEEN
KEEP THE HOME FIRES BURNING
Stephen
Winter, 1862

The South Carolina winter, such as it was, was also approaching. Although Nannook of the North was not expected to visit that area as obviously as he would visit northern Virginia, life on the plantation changed a little with the season. It was harder to get up in the morning, as the occasional nip in the air made the blankets feel pretty good. Stephen definitely had his hands full, as he attempted to keep the field hands operating. For leverage, he had only bluff, coercion, and the oft-used, "Do you really want an overseer back here over us?" The final cotton crop of the year was in process of being harvested. It looked like a bumper crop, in spite of all the obstacles which the self-motivated slaves had to hurdle.

Stephen talked to Miss Annie almost daily about the harvest and ultimate marketing of the crop. For the first time, Stephen learned about the selling part of the cotton business. He found that this was certainly not a normal time and selling the cotton was no longer as simple as it had been prior to the war. Miss Annie had to use all the connections she had, in order to find a buyer for the cotton, and even then, he was paying far less than in years past. The buyer's major problem was getting the cotton past the ocean blockades with which the Yankees were slowly but surely strangling commerce in the South. The buyer selected by Miss Annie had been very successful in running the blockades in the past. He planned to sell the cotton in the North, where prices were actually rising, if you could get it there without the baled crop being burned along with the ship.

Stephen had the problems of picking, baling and transporting the cotton on his mind, as he assembled the field hands on the first morning of picking. He looked around when he arrived at the assembly point, and for the second time in as many weeks, he counted two less field hands.

"Whar am Joe and George?" Stephen asked.

Nobody answered him. Stephen saw the downward cast and shifting eyes which usually signaled that the missing hands had cut and run.

"Don't matter, we kin do it ourselves, I reckon. We haz tuh, else dar will be no food or clothes dis winter fer us, iffen Miss Annie don't git her full crop in. Let's git movin cause we has tuh git sebbral rows picked today."

The hands walked toward the bottom lands that for many years had successfully produced cotton for the plantation. They swung into their day's work. By mid-day and Miss Annie's lunch time visit, the sun was bearing down with a vengeance on the workers, and winter seemed far away. Miss Annie's sharp eye noted the lesser number of slaves, and she walked over to Stephen.

"Did we have more runaways," she asked?

"I reckon so, meybe two, dat's all," responded Stephen. "Dar's still enuf ob us tuh git in de cotton, though Ize worried bout next spring and plantin. We be in trubble den, for shore."

"We'll worry about that next spring," said Miss Annie. "For now, we have to get this crop in within only a few weeks; otherwise the buyer will have to move out toward Europe. He heard that there are several more Yankee iron-sided ships steaming near the Atlantic coast down toward Charleston Harbor. That makes him and all the blockade runners very nervous, and he might not even take our cotton if those ships arrive and blockade running gets any more difficult than it already is."

"We'll git it dun, Miss Annie," vowed Stephen, "We somehow git it dun."

He muttered to himself as he walked back into the rows of cotton, stretching as far as the eye could see. He began picking with a vengeance. His enthusiasm was contagious and the hands on either side of him began moving more rapidly than their usual slow, deliberate motions of cotton-picking. On the next row, one of the hands began singing a hymn in rhythm to the faster picking, and most of the hands joined in.

By the end of the day, they surpassed the quota which they had set, and Stephen was elated. Now, if he could just do something to stem the increasing tide of runaways, they could meet Miss Annie's schedule. This would allow the cotton to be delivered to the ship in order to sell the crop. His brain began whirling. He thought as hard as he could about what he could do to keep the other field hands on the plantation. If his brothers, Nathan and James, who had always thought him to be slow, could observe the mental gyrations which their youngest brother was presently going through, they would be most impressed.

After the ritual washing up at the spring and the usual meal of cornbread, beans and bacon shared with Momma, Stephen gradually moved through the slave cabin clearing. He talked to as many of the field hands as were willing to listen to him. In all his thinking, he had not really come up with any fresh ideas on what seemed to be an insurmountable problem. As he talked with the other hands, he kept hoping for a miracle idea to suddenly appear in his head.

Stephen's pitch for now was the need for the plantation to have enough income so that all could eat that winter and at the same time, to fulfill their desire to have no overseer brought in. He said to one argumentative hand that freedom was apparently a wonderful thing, but you couldn't eat it, nor could you feed it to your wife and babies. After he completed his visits, Stephen went home for the night feeling the additional weight of discouragement. He wondered if he was wasting his time trying to convince the other field hands and he expressed his feelings of concern to Momma.

"Lordy, chile, you can't tell what a man be tinking inside his head! I reckon dat doze who gwine run, gwine run. You keep doin whut youze doin, and de good Lor will tek keer ob de rest."

Stephen, slightly mollified, went to bed, ready to face another hard day on the morrow. He remembered to say his prayers and added to the end of them, "Lor please takes keer ob Nathan and James, even tho dey gwine different ways. I hopes tuh see dem both when dis war am ober."

The slaves settled down to their self-imposed hard schedule. Stephen spent much of his days on mule back, going back and forth between the fields and the shed area where the cotton was being baled for shipment. Although the pressure stayed on from Stephen and the picking pace continued to be rapid, the rows of stacked cotton bales grew too slowly. The days flew by and Stephen was shocked one day when Miss Annie, during their now customary lunch discussion of how things were going, told Stephen that the selected buyer was planning to depart within the week and they had to be ready for him.

Stephen, in a surprised tone of voice responded, "But, Miss Annie, we won't be dun wid all de picking by den!"

"That's all right; we'll have most of it done, and it's better to successfully sell most of the crop than it would be to take a chance and try and pick it all," replied Annie. "You need to keep picking right to the last minute, and what we don't get baled and sent to the North, we'll hand gin that cotton ourselves like they used to do a few years ago and make more clothes for the Confederate Army and for ourselves."

Stephen went back to work eagerly, vowing to pick as much of the crop as possible. Once again, his energy was contagious, and the work pace of the field hands increased, over and above the already accelerated pace.

By the end of the week the planter, true to his word, sent a wagon train to pick up the baled cotton. Stephen was proud that the hands had picked and baled as much cotton in two weeks as they used to pick in four weeks. Miss Annie was equally delighted as she stood by the wagons and marked each bale of cotton on her slate as it was loaded.

"Well, Stephen, I guess we'll eat this winter after all, assuming the buyer manages to get through the blockades. How much more cotton is left on the plants, would you guess?"

"I reckon bout five hundred bales, counting the final pick on doze rows we already pick, Miss Annie. I kinda gots an idea, tho, dat I'd like tuh tell you."

"Go ahead," answered Miss Annie, "I told you last spring that I was always interested in your ideas. Now, what are you thinking?"

"Well, Miss Annie, I wuz tinking dat mebbe we could do several tings wit dat cotton lef on de plants."

As he started talking, Stephen was not really sure about where his idea was taking him. He paused for breath, then jumped back in with both feet. If ever there was a time for that miracle idea he had prayed for, this was that time.

"We could pick half ob de cotton for de Federacy and our clothes, and pick and bale de oder half and store it in de sheds."

Okay, so far so good. Miss Annie had already said basically the same thing. Now, what about the rest of the cotton. Let's see, how can we fix the runaway problem and get rid of the rest of the cotton at the same time? Then, it struck Stephen like the proverbial bolt of lightning out of the sky. He took one more deep breath and plunged in again.

"Miss Annie, you knows dat we forever hearin bout de blockade runners dat kin git thru de Yankee blockade and git across de ocean tuh England. Iffin we git half de rest ob dat cotton thru, we git top dollar for de cotton, an we all do better dis winter. Anyway, dat am my idea."

"Stephen that could work!" exclaimed Miss Annie. "When the blockade runners are active and there is a good market, they indeed pay top dollar, particularly when they can get to England. It's even more of a gamble, because those overseas blockade runners don't pay unless the cotton is sold and they get back, but it may be worth a chance. Let's do it!"

"Miss Annie," timidly started Stephen, as the rest of the lightning bolt solidified in his mind, "Does you tink maybe you could figger a way tuh hep out de field hands? Iffin dey git dis extra cotton picked and it git sold, mebbe a little reward ob some kind?"

Miss Annie was silent for a moment, and Stephen held his breath, feeling that maybe he was beginning to overstep his bounds. Silence hung between the two people for a moment; then Miss Annie responded.

"Stephen, I think that's a good idea. No, it's a great idea! It might help us a little in stemming the tide of runaways. Yes, I'll reward each of the field hands by giving them twenty dollars, if the blockade crop is successfully sold and we get paid. Do you want me to tell the hands about this plan?"

Stephen thought deeply for another moment, then took his final gamble. He had taken so many chances over the last few moments that surely one more wouldn't be too much.

"Miss Annie, iffin you doesn't mind, I'd kinda lik tuh tells dem myself, dis evening. Maybe it perk dem up, cause dey bin workin mighty hard dese las few weeks. But, Miss Annie, I wuz tinking--do you rekon you might gibs each ob dem thirty dollar, instead? Dat sound better an it mite makes a difference."

To Stephen's utter amazement, Miss Annie began laughing, harder and harder, until tears appeared on her cheeks, and she had to bend over and hold her side, as if she had a bad pain. Stephen had not seen any person laugh as hard as that, especially in the past several years.

"Lordy, Stephen, I'm not sure I can afford many more of your ideas," choked Miss Annie. "All right, thirty dollars it is. I believe that would be a good idea. Go ahead and tell them tonight about your plan."

She walked back toward the Big House, shaking her head. Stephen swore later when he was telling the story to Momma that he heard her still chuckling as she walked away. She left Stephen standing as if rooted, his mind awhirl. Your plan, she said, your plan! I reckon the rest of the hands will be mighty happy with that plan! I can hardly wait to tell them about that plan!

Stephen started singing as he walked back to the slave cabins, shouting at the top of his voice. Stephen's singing voice was not what could be called good, even when one was trying to be charitable.

Momma had said once, "Chile, it be a good ting dat de Lor lubs us for ourselves and our efforts, an not for our singin. Iffen not, I reckon you would be in trubble!"

Since Momma's eyes were about as bright as the North Star when she made this observation, Stephen laughed along with her and vowed to sing just as vigorously during church.

"I reckon dat iffen I do keeps on singin, de cows may quit givin milk and de chickens may quit laying in fright, but de good Lor will knows Ize still here!"

Feeling as if he were walking on air, Stephen somehow made it back to the clearing and thoroughly enjoyed his dinner with Momma.

"Chile, you looks lik a ant on a hot rock. What's you so cited bout, anyway?"

"I tells you after dinner," teased Stephen. "I gots someting dat all de field hands an dey families be cited bout!"

No amount of poking and prodding or even threatening by Momma could get anything else out of Stephen, and he stuck to his guns of telling no one until he told everyone. It was Momma's turn to be the ant on the hot rock.

After dinner, Stephen wandered out to the gathering log in the slave quarter clearing where the informal discussion sessions were held between dinner and dark. In a total break with tradition, Momma forwent her customary dish washing, left the dirty pots, and followed immediately behind Stephen. When the other field hands and their families saw Momma in the clearing, they figured something was up and began drifting in that direction. When Stephen saw that all the hands had collected he cleared his throat and began.

"Ize gots someting tuh tells you, someting dat Miss Annie telled me today. We is gwine tuh go back into de cotton fields startin tomorrow, and we iz gwine collect de res ob de cotton dat we didn't git fer de shipment tuh de North."

This announcement was greeted by loud groans from the slaves, who had visualized and hoped for several days of rest before their arduous field duties resumed.

"Dat's not all she tells me. She say dat we gwine use half ob dat cotton for clothes for us and fer de Federate Army."

More loud groans from the assembled field hands. Several started to loudly complain. Stephen held his hand up for silence, and to his amazement, the grumbling ceased and quiet returned to the clearing.

Stephen took a breath, then started with the rest of his plan. They hadn't lynched him so far, even though he had told them the bad news first. Now let's see how they react to the good news.

"Now, de oder half of dat cotton is gwine be baled, and is gwine be shipped on one ob de blockade-runnin ships tuh England fer sale. Iffen dat ship make it thru de blockade and Miss Annie git paid, she gwine gib each ob us field hands thirty dollars tuh use as we wants."

This announcement was greeted with a completely different response. The earlier groans and jeers turned into laughs, and buzzes of excited conversation broke out all over the clearing. Thirty dollars was four months' wages for a free man and a virtual fortune to a slave in 1863. There was a variety of ways that money could be used, especially if it was gold. The meeting broke up, and the excited slaves went to their cabins, still planning and dreaming what thirty dollars would buy.

Stephen was absolutely delighted at the immediate change in attitudes of the field hands. Before he and Momma dropped off to sleep that night, they also joined in the pastime of figuring what they could each do with thirty dollars.

The last thing Momma said before they went to sleep was, "I declare, chile, we each dun spended dat thirty dollar so many times dat we may need to git a bunch ob thirty dollars to cubber ebryting!"

Stephen laughed in agreement. Before he could come up with another way to spend money, he rolled over and fell asleep, enjoying a deep and dreamless sleep.

When the next day came, Stephen was amazed to find that not only were there no runaways, but there were a number of the slaves already in the fields picking cotton before he even got there. That was particularly a surprise, especially since he was normally the first out there. He was greeted cheerfully by those who saw him, and all the field hands settled down to work at a steady pace. Stephen was once again astonished at the end of the day, by the number of filled cotton bags which were loaded on the wagons, since much of the field being picked was the secondary crop. This cotton was left in the fields after the hands had already picked once. Miss Annie was there as well and was equally pleasantly surprised at the results which the reward promise had brought.

She smiled at Stephen and said, "I guess I don't have to ask if you told the other hands about the reward. It seems to be quite successful. I'd better begin looking for a blockade runner, one who has a good record of success."

The next few days and weeks passed uneventfully, and Stephen was proud that there were no runaways at all during the cotton-picking completion. It turned out that Stephen's estimation of the quantity of cotton left on the plants was a little short, and the field hands managed to collect some six hundred bales of cotton. The cotton was baled and after several days a man supervising a wagon train showed up at the plantation and hauled three hundred bales away.

Stephen and the other field hands settled in mentally to wait for the hoped-for return of the blockade runner a few months later. The routine on the plantation went back to normal and repair of tools, harnesses, and replacement of boards on sheds and barns were the order of the day as winter settled in on the South Carolina Low Country.

The only memorable occurrence happened one day when Miss Annie asked Stephen to accompany Cassie, the young pretty girl who lived next door to him, over to the next plantation. Miss Annie wanted Stephen to help Cassie pick up some material that the next door neighbor's wife had purchased from a friend who had traveled to the North before the war. The neighbor decided she needed money more than she needed to keep all of the material, so Miss Annie convinced her to sell enough material for two or three new dresses for herself and her daughters.

Stephen found as the two rode together on the old mule that it became easier and easier to talk to Cassie. By the time they returned home and he had deposited Cassie and the material at the Big House, they had become good friends. They excitedly talked about how life was different now and how it would be even more different after the war, whatever way it went. Stephen made a decision. Even before the war ended, he would try to get Cassie for his wife, and he vowed to ask her first chance he got.

CHAPTER FOURTEEN
THE PACE INCREASES
James
Spring-Summer, 1863

Life in the First South Carolina Volunteers for James droned along during the first part of 1863, with more drills, lots of marching, and considerable equipment cleaning and repairing.

James once said to Joseph, "Iffen I cleans dis stuff eny mor, dar won't be no leather lef, nuttin but spit an polish."

However, toward the end of May, the activity began to pick up. The word spread among the troops of the First South Carolina that the soldiers were about to be joined on the islands by a substantial Union fighting force, the Fifty-fourth Massachusetts Volunteers. That regiment, like their own, was made up entirely of black volunteer soldiers led by young white officers.

The Fifty-fourth arrived at Beaufort on Port Royal Island near the headquarters of the First South Carolina Volunteers. James and several others in the First South asked for and received permission to go see the arrival and disembarking of the Fifty-fourth.

It was truly a grand arrival, as the well-drilled, well-uniformed soldiers marched off the steamer and onto the docks of Beaufort. James felt a real surge of pride as he watched the gleaming black faces of the marching soldiers. In a "moment of madness" which he could not explain, he worked his way through the crowd until near one of the white officers of the fighting unit. The officer turned around and saw James's uniform, saluted. and was saluted in turn.

The officer asked James, "What unit are you with, soldier?"

James responded, "De Fus Souf Carolina, Lieutenant. We be headquartered on de next island. We been making a few raids on plantations up river, but we ain't really fight any Secesh yet."

The lieutenant informed James that the Fifty-fourth, indeed, was slated to participate in major battles in the near future and asked him, "Say, soldier, who is your commanding officer?"

"It be Cunnel Higginson, Suh," responded James.

"When you go back to your camp, please ask the colonel to come see my commanding officer. We're in need of a few soldiers to fill out our ranks; we lost a few to desertion when it was announced that we were headed for battle. I think that my commander would very much like to talk to Colonel Higginson."

James agreed to speak to his colonel. He saluted smartly again and returned to stand with the other soldiers of the First South that had come with him to Beaufort. During their walk back to their camp, he excitedly talked about the Lieutenant's request with the other members of the First South as they walked back across the wooden bridge to their island.

James went directly to his colonel, who thanked him for bringing the message. He said he would visit Beaufort the next day and talk to the officer. James then forgot about the request. However, it kept nagging him in a small corner of his memory that night. Before the colonel left the next day, James went back to him, saluted, and requested, "Colonel, I'd lik to be one of dose goin to de Fifty-fourth, if dat's whut de officer wuz gwine ask."

"I'll consider your request, soldier," responded the colonel as he rode off toward Beaufort.

When the colonel returned later that day, he immediately retired into his headquarters tent and called for the first sergeant. The two men stayed in the tent for about an hour. They came out and called for the bugler to sound assembly.

The Colonel stood in front of the men for a minute, then began, "Men, this, the First South Carolina Volunteers, is a good unit. Maybe even a great unit. You men have joined together in spite of unbelievable odds and have acquitted yourselves well in our forays across this countryside. You all know the Fifty-Fourth Massachusetts arrived yesterday at Beaufort, and their commanding officer has asked me to provide him with ten of my soldiers to fill out a company that lost several men to desertion on the way down here from the North.

The Fifty-Fourth is an impressive unit, and it looks like they will be used in a major battle very soon. The work we of the First South are doing here is important. We've kept the Secessionists off-balance by our raids, and we expect to continue doing the same for the remainder of the war. Sergeant Washington and I have compiled a list of the ten men who we feel would best serve our country by this transfer. I'll call the names, and if any of the men so chosen do not desire to be transferred, come and see the sergeant, and we'll select another soldier."

He read nine names, and James began feeling very badly, as none of the nine were his. Finally, after a pause, the colonel looked at James, and called his name. James felt immediate relief, mixed with pride and even a little bit of fright. He was in! He was going to be able to fight the Confederates and help gain his permanent freedom. Not just temporary, as he felt that his current freedom was, but forever! James hunted up Joseph after the assembly and told him his reasons for the transfer.

Joseph seemed to understand, and the two men briefly hugged as they parted company. James went to his tent and began packing his equipment, as the transferees were told that they would be leaving the next day for the Fifty-fourth.

The ten men left for Beaufort early the next morning, accompanied by their sergeant. The frightened transfers were greeted by a staff sergeant of the Fifty-Fourth and were taken to a supply tent and outfitted with the uniform of the Regiment. They were re-sworn in and assigned to Company F, where they were immediately lined up.

The drill sergeant proceeded to tell them at the top of his voice, that all of them were truly country bumpkins, few of them knew their right feet from their left, and all of them undoubtedly knew absolutely nothing. He, the sergeant, as much as he regretted it, would have to work very hard to bring them up to the standards of the Fifty-Fourth before any of them would be allowed to be seen in public.

The sergeant regretted all of the extra time and effort that this work was going to cause him personally, and he was not betting on success. He said that he felt bad about all of that extra work, and any and all of them would regret causing him to have to do it. James felt a tug of loyalty for the First South and all of the drilling that had been done and the improvement that they had shown. He smartly decided that this was not the place for a response. If they could show this city soldier what the transfers were capable of, then maybe he would recognize the worth of their former unit.

James and the other nineteen members of Company F began what proved to be the longest four weeks of their entire lives. The sergeant constantly verbally harassed them and drilled them day and night. He marched them to meals, church, and even to the latrine. James felt a surge of pride in the improvement the unit was showing in drilling and marching over the four weeks. Marching to the latrine instead of running when one had "soldiers' revenge," was a way to gain some measure of humility and self-control. James had to admit that, perhaps, this city boy knew exactly what he was doing in preparing his troops for battle.

Early in July, Company F was lined up along the rest of the Fifty-Fourth, and all of the soldiers were given orders to move out. The soldiers were to be force-marched to the little town of Darien, Georgia, on the coast just down from Beaufort, and there, they were to completely destroy and burn the town. James felt a little pain and discomfort, as this was what he had been doing with the First South, and was not what he had transferred to do.

As they did their work of destruction, James and his comrades became even more unhappy as they heard the fruitless pleading of the people of Darien asking the soldiers to spare their homes. The soldiers made an attempt to save the houses in the black section of Darien, small tumble-down shacks much like their own at home. Unfortunately, the winds spread the roaring flames from the other parts of Darien, and the whole town was reduced to ashes by the raging conflagration. James felt real stirrings in his conscience, and these feelings were shared by the rest of the soldiers. Nevertheless, the Fifty-Fourth did exactly what the troops were ordered to do. They left nothing but smoldering ruins in their wake as they returned to Beaufort that evening.

Even though Darien was of minor military importance as an occasional port, the soldiers were not happy about making war on civilians. However, James and the others talked and agreed that the day's exercise was to make the regiment work better as a unit, and perhaps they would be really fighting soon. James and his fellow soldiers definitely hoped so. Even though trashing plantations could be satisfying because of the problems it caused the Secesh, it was also hard on the slaves who lived on those plantations who had no place to go once their homes were burned. James had managed to talk to a few of them and directed them towards the First South and some decided to join up with that unit.

The rumors began flying over the next two weeks that the Fifty-fourth was about to be involved in a large-scale operation, perhaps to try to retake Fort Wagner from the Confederates. It turned out that the rumors had accurately predicted the future, as on July 16, the soldiers left James Island, and the Fifty-fourth had a short skirmish against a few scattered Confederate troops. They then went to Coles Island, marching across the small wooden bridge which connected the two barrier islands. From there, the Fifty-fourth embarked for Folly Island early on the morning of July 18. The Fifty-fourth marched to the northern end of that island, and were next ferried to Morris Island where testing time was to come.

The soldiers of the unit were unaware of the vicious political battles that had been fought in Washington, D.C. on their behalf. Many citizens, even some of the top officers of the military, felt strongly that the black soldiers were only able to provide support for the white troops, digging trenches, latrines, and foxholes, handling supplies, and the like. Everyone knew that the colored troops were not really capable of fighting against, much less of defeating white troops. This excursion would tell the tale, and the black soldiers were quite anxious to acquit themselves like men. The impending assault on Fort Wagner, if and when successful, would send a message, loud and clear, to the disbelievers and detractors of the colored troops, and every member of the Fifty-fourth swore to take a major part in changing opinions.

That night, James and three privates in the Fifty-fourth sat around their campfire. They sang songs, first the patriotic songs of the day, then reverted to Negro spirituals. James possessed a fine baritone voice and he joined with great gusto in the singing. Silence fell, although they could still hear singing going on around similar campfires.

James spoke. "I be a bit afraid bout tomorrow. Mos of our fightin so far, dere bin nobuddy shootin at us. Wat you tink we gonna do when dey start wid cannon and guns a'shootin at us?"

The other three stayed quiet. The silence hung over the campfire. Thoughts were racing through four heads and no one wanted to speak what was on their mind.

One man finally looked up from the campfire where his eyes had been glued.

"I'm afraid, too. I reckon I can say that like you did, James. I wants to live like everything cause I got a wife and two children back in Massachusetts state. Even though we're free up North, the white folks sure don't treat us like they do each other. I reckon that's one reason I'm down here. Maybe if we do fight good tomorrow, the white folks will treat us better."

Silence again prevailed around the campfire, which served not only to provide light and warmth, but also provided a sense of security, wrapping the four frightened men in its warm glow.

The other two men confessed that in spite of their brave facades and boasts of what they would do to the Rebs when they finally faced them, they were afraid inside. Afraid for their own safety and afraid the unit would prove unworthy and panic in the face of the enemy.

James spoke up again. "I rekon dats why we be here. De officers wants dat fort, but I reckon de temper of de Fifty-fourth gwine be tested in de fire of battle. I member at home at de blacksmith's forge how de steel seemed to suffer as it be made red-hot ober de fire, den de smithy beat on it wid a hammer. Onct de temper am proved and de shoe be dropped in de barrel ob water, it come out mity strong. I reckon dat's whut gwine happen tomorrow to us. De Fifty-fourth gwine be tested. We haz to come out of de odder side stronger, dat's all. We haz to!"

Nods of agreement around the fire signified agreement with what James had said. Murmurs of resolution punctuated the silence, and the men gradually drifted away to their tents. There they would lie awake for hours, thinking their private thoughts and facing their private dragons before they were able to sleep, to prepare for tomorrow. Tomorrow promised to test the temper of themselves, the Massachusetts Fifty-fourth and maybe even impact all Negroes. The weight on each man's shoulders was considerable.

At seven-thirty in the morning, the troops of the Massachusetts Fifty-fourth marched toward Fort Wagner. The fort was in a nearly impenetrable location. The route the soldiers would take included several obstacles, including a short march through sea water at a narrow part of the spit, up a small hill, and then next through a ditch containing four feet of water slowly flowing over a foot or two of black marsh mud, known as gumbo. When a man's feet contacted the gumbo, his shoes were immediately covered with mud and each foot weighed many pounds.

The Fifty-fourth broke ranks to get through the obstacles which were located only a few hundred feet from the fort. Amazingly enough, no fire had come from the fort yet. The Southern defenders of the fort were waiting for the Union troops to get within a closer range.

Ultimately the colored troops had to break ranks and reform after crossing the ditch. Then, a rain of bullets began to fall on the soldiers. A large percentage of the troops fell, but many more found their way forward, James among them. They slogged through the mud, feeling the pull and tug of the suction on their feet. This was particularly frustrating, trying to run hard for protection from soldiers firing down on them, and being able to barely lift their feet off the ground.

James felt the pluck of a bullet on his uniform sleeve, and the sting on his arm told him that he had been slightly wounded. He ignored the sharp pain and continued to run through the dark, stinking clouds of smoke toward the parapets of the fort, along with several dozen men.

The Fifty-fourth fired at shadowy figures on the parapets, then dropped to one knee to reload, then charged again. James saw one shadowy figure fall as he fired a shot in his direction. About a dozen men of the Fifty-fourth made it to the sloping side of the fort and faced another withering fire as the survivors continued upward. James felt the pain in his left leg as a Minie' ball struck him directly on the leg below the knee. He couldn't ignore this pain; it was too great. He fell to the ground and cried out in agony. As he lay there unsure of what to do next, the color sergeant in front of him screamed and fell, pierced by a dozen bullets at once, splattering his life-blood on James and those few other soldiers around him.

James without thinking, scrambled to his feet, and dragging his wounded leg, lunged forward and reached for the flag. He planted it on top of the slope and clung to the flag standard, standing on one leg. The surviving men ahead of James continued forward, fighting hand-to-hand with the Confederate defenders. James was hit by another bullet in his upper arm, but he clutched the flag even tighter and was only able to scream in defiance at the figures which he could barely see. The bullets flew again, and this time, several of them struck James in the chest, and he fell, lifeless, at the foot of the flag and the uniform he was so proud to wear was completely torn and bloodied.

The hand-to-hand fighting, even though it gave every indication of hours, lasted only about ten minutes, until there were but a handful of the Union invaders left alive. As help was clearly not forthcoming, the few survivors were forced to fall back. One of the retreating men spotted James curled around the flag standard, holding it still upright surrounded by his body. The man tugged, and pulled the flag loose, and he carried it with him as he retreated. The Fifty-Fourth had lost 247 men, more than the entire Confederate force had lost.

The survivors of the bloody battle were ferried back to Beaufort. Stories of the brave assault, even though unsuccessful in its goal to re-take the fort, were told and retold around the campfires and in Washington. Joseph came up from the island headquarters of the First South and learned that James was one of the men who had fallen and was buried by the Confederates, along with the white Yankee officers, in a mass grave in front of the fort. As he wiped a tear from his eye at the loss of his friend, he listened closely to the tale of one of the survivors. The more he listened to the story of the soldier who managed to keep the flag upright with his body, even after crossing the line over into death, the more intrigued he was. He asked the soldier about who the heroic soldier might have been.

The man said, "I believe his name was James--he used to be with a South Carolina unit. He was truly a brave man."

Joseph replied in a choking voice, "He were dat, but eben more portant, he died free--really free! Dat's what I will tells his Momma and his brudders when next I sees dem. James had a true cullud man's heart."

Joseph went back to the First South Carolina Volunteers and repeated again and again the story of James's brave actions and his death, and all who listened were touched. The question of whether or not the colored troops were capable of being brave soldiers and could fight on a par with the white soldiers was laid to rest, along with the 247 dead of the Massachusetts Fifty-fourth, buried in a common grave along with their officers in the sands of Fort Wagner.

☐ ☐ ☐ ☐

CHAPTER FIFTEEN
ANOTHER SPRING
Nathan
Spring-Summer, 1864

The spring of 1864 found the Holcombe Legion still encamped in northern Virginia. The activities of the winter had been similar to what the Legion had done in the winters of the past two years. The Legion made occasional brief forays into the countryside and engaged the enemy in minor skirmishes, but nothing major. The Legion sustained a few wounded; several men were sent home to recover, but no one was killed.

Will had his horse shot out from under him during one skirmish, but rolled out from under the falling animal. Aside from a few scrapes, he was not badly injured. He was luckily able to buy a horse from a neighboring farm. This part of the country had been crossed and re-crossed by both armies numerous times. The farmers had hidden their favorite horses so the Yankees couldn't find them, but they were willing to sell a horse to a son of the South. However, there was precious little livestock of any kind left on any of the farms.

Nathan and Will gained an even closer relationship as the two worked together every day, and each knew what the other was about to say before they said it. There were not very many body servants left with the unit now. Most of them, like Nathan, had been freed by their masters and were now paid servants. These remaining men were completely loyal and a real part of the Holcombe Legion, even as much as the soldiers.

With the advent of spring, the Legion was once again loaded onto a train and moved south toward Richmond, then marched to the west of the city. The unit, along with a substantial Southern contingency, played cat-and-mouse with Yankee troops. They finally came together in battle in a place which neither army wanted. The area was known locally as the Wilderness, for good reason. For several days, the two armies stumbled through the near-zero visibility brush and forest, killing tremendous numbers on both sides.

Just about as many soldiers were killed by fires started by rifle muzzle flash as were killed by direct hits from bullets. Nathan found that keeping Will's spirits in good shape during this awful battle was more difficult than it had been at any other time during the long war. Discussions with other servants disclosed that their masters and employers were in the same frame of mind.

All levels of the military on both sides, from commanding generals down to the lowliest private, were equally glad when the engagement was finally broken off, without a declared winner.

Will remarked to Nathan as they left the area, "I'll be truly glad to be able to see the enemy I am fighting again. This battle has been tougher on us than any we've fought so far. We can't see them, but we can hear them scream. There's no honor in such a fight. No honor at all."

Nathan had to agree. "I haz handled so many charred folk de las few days I thought I wuz in de smokehouse, back on de plantation. Dey was in pain and dey wuz nuttin we could do fer them. Iffin a man bin shot, you kin hep him a bit wid de pain, but not fer dem burns. I reckon dat I nebber be able to forgit dis place, effin I wants to. I believes my nose not gwine be able to ebber forgit de smell of charred meat or de sound of screamin, not ebber."

The men lapsed into a companionable silence, each hurting inside and hurting for the other man. For the first time, Nathan also sensed that Will was becoming extremely discouraged with the war effort, and his optimism for an ultimate victory was shrinking. Even the long-expected promotion to captain that Will received did not help his spirits. Nathan was nevertheless prouder of his friend than ever before.

Nathan and Will had several conversations about what life on the plantation would be like after the war. Nathan noticed that Will never talked about the situation of the slaves on the place. Will did mention that he had heard from his mother and that a number of the slaves had fled, but Stephen was doing quite well as an ad hoc overseer. Nathan's Momma was still the same, acting as Momma or Auntie to all the people on the plantation, black and white alike. Nathan was surprised and delighted at the news about Stephen, as he had found his place and had flowered with sibling rivalry no longer a handicap.

Speculations and discussions about what was to happen stopped with a screech as the Legion was called into action at Petersburg, a small Southern city right below Richmond, Virginia. Petersburg was the key to the Yankee goal of capturing the Confederate capital of Richmond. The Legion was slipped into the fortified Southern lines under the cover of darkness and took up residence in a section of the awesome breastworks which had been slave-constructed to protect Petersburg.

Days stretched into weeks and then into months. The two armies parried and thrust, and there was little success or progress on either side. As this was the first siege situation he had seen, Nathan queried Will one day about what was being accomplished.

Will told him, "As I understand the situation, our army isn't strong enough here to make a real attack on the Union Army. The Yankees are two or three times our strength. We're strong enough because we're behind these breastworks. We can hold them off indefinitely, at least as long as we can get supplies. We're hoping to wait them out, and maybe the Yanks will get discouraged and move on. Then we can attack them while they're not in such a strong position and their soldiers can be strung out."

The siege at Petersburg did drag on and on, but the Legion got a reprieve, of sorts. The soldiers were ordered out of Petersburg, further weakening an already-weak portion of the thin gray line. The Union forces had gradually but surely stretched the line by moving their superior forces further around the city, forcing the Confederate defenders to continue to front them to avoid being "rolled up". This action resulted in making the defense line even thinner and in some places defenders could hardly see the next soldiers down the line, they were so far apart.

The Legion was ordered back to South Carolina, specifically to the Charleston area. They were to defend that city against the threat posed by a rumored Southern campaign led by Union General William Tecumseh Sherman, through Georgia and next maybe turning east and north through South Carolina. As South Carolina had led the secessionist movement, the men, both black and white, knew that retribution in the state would be swift and terrible. The Legion members had mixed feelings, as they knew their home state needed protection, but the soldiers also knew that their absence would make already beleaguered Petersburg and ultimately Richmond even more vulnerable.

The Legion departed the way it had come, under the cloak of darkness. Safely leaving the city and moving south around the Union lines, the officers, soldiers, servants, and assorted aides once again loaded onto a train and were transported south and east to Charleston. As an old hand at train travel by now, Nathan no longer felt any hesitation about climbing on the car pulled by the iron horse. After the hundreds of miles he had ridden and walked during the course of the war, the train trip was a much preferred alternative.

Arriving in Charleston a few days later, the weary Legion was greeted by the local residents with great expressions of relief. Nathan, however, received a different type of welcome. From the colored people on the street, he received looks which could hardly be construed as friendly. He tried to speak to several people, and the blacks refused to talk, scurrying away with great alacrity like the fiddler crabs that abounded in the shallow estuaries of the Charleston area.

Nathan, after asking around, received the same reaction from all blacks, whether slave or free. This disturbed him greatly, as he had always prided himself as being able to get along with almost anyone. He talked to the rest of the servants in his company and found that all had received the same treatment. They were as puzzled and concerned as he was, and they decided to try to solve the dilemma.

The servants sent several of their number with Nathan as spokesman to the commander of the Legion and presented their problem. He told them there was a tremendous problem with the slaves and the recently-freeded slaves in that area, as many had been freed by Union advances in the area. The confused and starving contrabands had nowhere to go. Many of them found their way to Charleston where they were not distinguishable from the colored people of that area, and many caused trouble.

The colonel advised the servants still attached to the Holcombe Legion to travel only in groups and be especially cautious when encountering unknown people in the vicinity of the camp.

The assembled body servants agreed to take this safe approach but they expressed a reluctance to report any of these people to the authorities. The colonel understood their feelings but warned them again to be cautious. The servant representatives returned to their camp, maybe as confused as they were prior to their discussion with the commander.

Several additional body servants fled the camp over the next few weeks, preferring the uncertainties of the free life in Charleston to the more or less certain meals, clothing, and shelter of the servant or slave life in the Confederate Army. Nathan was saddened by these departures. Many of these men had become his close friends over the past three years. However, as some of their masters had not yet seen fit to free them as Will had freed him, he fully understood their feelings, and he silently wished them luck in their new lives.

Other than the newly created diversions, life in the Legion went along pretty much as normal. Nathan actually had it easy. Will, who knew many people in Charleston from his days at the Citadel, spent considerable time visiting friends when his duties with the Legion permitted. Other than keeping Will's now threadbare uniforms presentable, Nathan had substantial free time. However, the first day he decided to wander around the lower part of the city, he ran into trouble.

As he was passing a group of Confederate soldiers, one of them turned and stopped Nathan. "Hey, nigger, whar do you think you're going? We got work for you—come along with us: you're fixin tuh dig breastworks. Move!"

"But, Massuh," Nathan began in protest.

The soldier raised his rifle and swung it, hitting Nathan a solid blow on the side of the head, knocking him down.

Nathan, dazed and bleeding, tried again, "But Massuh, Ize a freemen, not a slave! Ize part of de Holcombe Legion of de Federacy."

One of the soldiers of cooler head stopped the first man from hitting Nathan again. "All right, nigger, can you prove you're a freeman and not a damned contraband?"

"Yassuh, here's my paper from my former Massuh, saying it." Nathan pulled out the tattered letter from Will that stated he was freed. The soldiers read it.

The second soldier said, "Damn, John, his master's an officer with the Army--you're in for it, now! Let's get the hell out of here!"

The soldiers threw the paper back at Nathan and sprinted away with great speed, leaving Nathan sprawled and bleeding on the street.

An ancient Negro lady happened by and helped Nathan to his feet, clucking like an old Momma hen, all the while.

"Here, baby, let me heps you. Dat sojer dun bashed you head in, dat's what he dun."

She wiped off the blood which had trickled down Nathan's face and helped half-drag and half-carry him down the street and through an alley to her ramshackle shipping crate home. She lay Nathan on his back on her own bed and started clucking again. "Auntie gwine bandage you head and fix you some hot soup. Dat will hep you feels better."

Before she could start on the soup, Nathan gave her his name and told her where Will was and that she should send someone to tell him what had happened. She covered Nathan with a tattered blanket, and scurried away.

Nathan fell back on the bed and promptly passed out. When he awoke, he was in a different place, in a bed with sheets, and his head was wrapped up in a large white bandage. He tried to rise, but the effort was too much for him; his head started spinning and he fell back.

An orderly stepped up to the bed and said, "Well, it seems you've finally decided to come back to us. Just lay back there for a while until your head feels better. I'll send word to the captain that you've come around, and maybe he'll stop pestering us four times a day and driving us crazy."

Nathan obeyed, and the orderly left. He returned a little while later with Will in tow.

"Nathan, welcome back! We were afraid that you weren't going to make it, but it seems you have the hard head I've always accused you of having," said Will, in a joking tone. "When that old Mammy found me four days ago, she said that a soldier had almost killed you, and when we went to pick you up, we were afraid that he had succeeded! We've hunted for the man that did this, but we haven't had any luck so far. We'll find him!"

Nathan feebly replied, "Dat be allrite, Mister Will; he didn't know Ize a free man. I guess I needs tuh start carryin a sign sayin dat."

"Well, let's not worry about that for now. Let's worry instead about getting you well and back on your feet again. I'm tired of washing my uniforms!" responded Will, again in a joking tone he used to disguise his worry about Nathan.

"Yassuh, I feels better already, and dey takin good keer ob me here. Dis bed a lot better dan de bedroll in my tent an I doezn't haz to cook my dinner."

Nathan fell back to sleep. Will looked down on him for long moments, both relieved at Nathan's responsiveness and pleased that he had apparently not suffered any brain damage from the hard blow to the head. He gently covered Nathan with the blanket and tiptoed out of the room.

It took a full week for the occasional dizzy spells to leave Nathan and he was able to return to his tent. He found himself being babied by Will.

"But, Mister Will, Ize all rite now. Ize sposed tuh tek keer ob you, not de odder way around," protested Nathan with very little conviction in his voice.

"Hush, Nathan, let me take care of you for a while, until you're completely over the blow. It won't hurt you!"

Nathan allowed as how he was sometimes still a little bit weak and dizzy, and he lay back down on his cot. He slept off and on for the next few days. When he announced that he was ready and able to return to his full duties, Will acquiesced.

Will told Nathan, "I rather enjoyed taking care of you after all the times you've cared for me. But, the one thing I did draw the line on was your sock washing business. I'm afraid the socks outside are lined up for quite a stretch. There're a lot of soldiers not wearing socks around here who will be ecstatic that you're back and in business again."

The Legion remained in Charleston for several months. They had few duties, other than guard duty and continuing to strengthen the defenses. Both the military and civilian representatives fully expected the Union Army to attack by either land or sea, or both. One day, Will came back to camp with a very serious look on his face.

He sat on the log where Nathan was resting and began, "Nathan, I really don't know how to begin to tell you this, but I'm afraid I've some very bad news for you. I was talking today with an officer assigned to one of the other units in town. They had just moved up here from Fort Wagner, over on the coast. The soldiers recently had the experience of a pitched battle against the first colored Union troops that they'd ever seen. The man I was talking to told me the colored soldiers were as brave as any soldiers he had ever seen. Even though the Yankees weren't able to take the fort, the colored troops fought ferociously and were able to gain the top slope of the wall of Fort Wagner before being pushed back and away from the fort.

The Southern officers were telling stories about a particularly brave young soldier who made it to the top of the wall and then grabbed their battle flag as it was falling. He planted the flag on top of the wall and defended it with his own body, even after suffering mortal wounds. Nathan, that brave soldier was your brother, James. He was serving with the Fifty-Fourth Massachusetts. Even though he was fighting for the enemy, soldiers always recognize true bravery and these men said your brother was truly a brave soldier."

Nathan felt a small tear escape from his eye and run down his cheek. He stood perfectly still for a moment, then gulped and said, "I will miss James, dat's for sho. He always wanbe free mo dan ennyting. I reckon he's free now. I'm glad dat he died a good sojer, and I tank you fer tellin me bout him. I hope dat you doesn't hold de fact dat he wuz a Union sojer agin him."

Will felt several tears trickle down his own cheeks and he felt a powerful empathy as he watched Nathan proudly walk out of camp. Nathan sat on a bench overlooking the water. Will thought about following him for a moment, then reasoned Nathan needed to be alone with his thoughts at that time.

Later that evening, Nathan came back to Will and asked, "Mister Will, could you see dat my Momma find out bout James being a good sojer an all? It would mean a lot tuh her and Stephen if dey knowed dat he did good. Don hold it again him dat he wuz always wantin tuh be free. We knowed as slaves how lucky we wuz dat you wuz our Massuhs. We preciate how you, yore Momma and Poppa and yore sisters allays bringed us extra food an clothes and how your Momma ebben teached some ob us tuh read a little. Iffin we all be free after de war, we needs tuh know how tuh do dat."

"I'll be glad to let your Momma and brother know about James's death," responded Will. "I'll direct a message to be sent as soon as possible, and I'll have my mother personally take the message down to your momma and stay for a while to help. I'd also like to do something else. What you say about reading and writing is exactly right. I know you can read only a little bit. Would you mind if I started working with you in the evenings when our schedules allow, to teach you how to read and write? I think you'll need those skills after the war, regardless who eventually wins, because you're still going to be a free man whether the Confederacy or the Union wins this awful war."

Nathan didn't have to think long at all before he responded with an eager, "Oh, yes, Mister Will. Dat would be fine, fer sho! Dere's no way I could be on my own widout being able tuh do both does tings. I would preciate it iffen you would heps me. Iffn it would't be too sumpious ob me, deres two odder servants dat am near dis tent, who has been freed, an dey needs tuh know de same tings. Do you reckon you could hep dem as well?"

Will laughed, and said, "I didn't know I was going into the schoolmaster business, but if their officers don't mind, I'll be glad to help them. We'll hold lessons every evening that we're able to, starting tomorrow. I need time to try and get a few books to teach with."

"Tanks, Mister Will, I preciate dat. Does you mind iffin I goes and tells de oder servants what you haz said?"

"No, of course not," said Will, pleased that the prospect of learning to read and write had temporarily taken Nathan's mind off his brother's death. "If their Masters have any problem with their servants joining the class, I'll talk to them tomorrow, and we'll work it out. It'll be easier for all of us if there are several students so you can help each other with the lessons as I give them to you."

So, the establishment that was to be known in the Holcombe Legion as Will's Little Schoolhouse was born. Nathan outdid himself, as a total of five ex-slaves, now freemen, showed up at Will's tent the next night. Will first scratched his head at his shortage of teaching materials. He decided to begin by having the men learn the alphabet and numbers.

Will had barely enough writing paper and writing quills and ink for each man to use, and he promised to try to enlist the supply sergeant's help the next day. He began by slowly forming each letter on a piece of paper, saying it, and having the men repeat it after him over and over again. He then looked over each man's shoulder as he laboriously wrote A, next B, and so forth.

Will proved to be an extremely patient teacher, as he spent more time on the slower learners, yet kept the quicker students challenged and interested. After about two hours, they had progressed through the letter K, and Will pronounced class over for the night. Nathan left feeling proud of himself, and all five promised to be back tomorrow.

For the next three nights, the class not only retained its original members, but grew by one each day. Will finally had to put a stop to the growth of the class. He was having a problem convincing the supply sergeant that he really needed as much paper and as many pens as he was requisitioning. The sergeant remarked that he couldn't believe how many official orders and letters home Will must be writing.

The morale of the men in the class stayed very high. Even though the studies were tough for some of the men, the eager students all kept plugging away, and the class progressed through the alphabet, the numbers, and then on to simple words. The students learned cat, dog, mother, father, etc.

The men in the class were really disappointed on the evenings when duty kept Will from teaching or them from learning. Will jokingly complained about what the class was doing to his social life, but he was just as proud of each man as the students mastered a new word as they were of themselves.

Will was having a challenge obtaining beginning reading books for texts, until one day, the local preacher came to camp to save souls. He had several boxes full of religious tracts, and he was impressed when Will asked him for at least ten copies of each different tract. When pressed for an explanation of why so many, Will stated that he was giving them away to "thirsty souls."

The class had not been widely publicized or discussed, as it was still against the law in the South to teach slaves to read or write. Will was not sure enough of the finer points of the law to say whether that law applied to ex-slaves or freedmen or not, but he took no chances. He did not say that the souls he mentioned were thirsty for learning, whatever the subject. So, the slaves learned about all types of sinning, as the eager students learned the use of words. The tracts were pocket-sized, simply written, and only a few pages long. The eager students addressed such subjects as conversion, how to seek religion, how to avoid certain sins, practical advice on health of body or soul and even how to avoid procrastination.

In addition to learning how to use words and how to put them together, the Negroes learned much about how the white Southerners felt about religion in the 1860's. Most of the ex-slaves were religious, and many of the South Carolinians were baptized Episcopalians and either had their own churches or attended their white masters' church on the plantation, although usually seated in the balcony.

The classes continued, and Will remained pleased with his students. He was also proud of the fact that he did not have to encourage or push the students at all. Each and every one of them was quite strongly self-motivated.

Will felt that the crowning success of the teaching was the morning he sat Nathan down at the writing desk with a clean sheet of paper and a new quill. He had Nathan write a letter home to his Momma and Stephen. Nathan told them what he had been doing for the past several years and how slow the war was for them at that time. Nathan closed the letter with a plea that, even though this letter would have to be read to them by Will's Mother, Stephen and Momma should learn to read and write, as they were going to need these skills after the war. The letter was printed in large, block letters, and signed with a flourish by Nathan at the bottom.

Will sent the letter home, enclosed in a letter to his mother with an explanation of what he had been doing for the past several months with the ex-slaves. Will's mother, Miss Annie, read, re-read, then re-read again the letter to Stephen and Momma, until both of them knew it by heart. The letter became a keepsake that Nathan's Momma carried with her for years after the war, until the document finally completely fell apart at the creases from being folded and unfolded so many times.

The Holcombe Legion enjoyed the respite from fighting, although food and supplies were scarce in Charleston primarily due to the success the Union blockades were enjoying. They knew, however, that the welcome rest time would end, and perhaps primary on each of the soldiers' minds was the hope that they would not lose their lives in the closing battles of the war, particularly as the outcome was all but settled. The understanding that the South was going to lose the war had slowly and painfully been realized by most of the soldiers except for the real die-hards. Many men had deserted, but most hung firm, prepared to fight to the last.

☐ ☐ ☐ ☐

CHAPTER SIXTEEN
THE HOME FRONT GETS TOUGHER
Stephen
Fall-Winter, 1864

On the plantation, the situation steadily became grimmer. Supplies from the outside, particularly food and clothing, became exceedingly scarce. Stephen and Momma received the bad news of James's death in the letter from Will to his mother, and they took it hard. The two mourners became local heroes as the relatives of a man who had died a conspicuous hero in battle. Slaves from neighboring plantations when visiting, took the time to look up Momma and Stephen and let them know how proud they were of what James had done.

One visitor brought a tattered newspaper clipping from the Boston Herald which had been smuggled in a letter. The story in the clipping was about the Battle of Fort Wagner. The story mentioned James by name and told what he had done to keep the flag from falling into the hands of the enemy. The attention and the expressions of sympathy helped ease the loss, and as planting season once again wore on, life on the plantation returned to normal.

Stephen had to turn his attention to other things, as runaways once again became a problem. The once large pre-war force of plantation field hands of more than one hundred men and women had shrunk to less than thirty. Stephen was hard pressed to get the planting done. The field hands planted cotton and corn in only one-half as many fields as had been planted in the past, but still managed to get them done.

One day, in the middle of the morning Miss Annie rode into the field where Stephen was working. She appeared to be quite excited, but would only say, "Stephen, I'd like you to come to the Big House this evening after work for the day is over and I'll give you my news then."

Stephen spent much of the rest of the day worrying about why he was being called to the Big House. When work ended, he rushed to wash up and hug Momma. He rode the old mule to the house at top speed, such as it was. He even passed up supper. When he arrived at the Big House, he was met at the door by one of the house servants. He was escorted into the office, the room that had been Old Master Richard's. Miss Annie now used that room to run the business of the plantation.

"Come in, Stephen," she said, "I have some good news in the midst of so much daily bad news. I received the word that, somehow, the blockade runner who was carrying our extra cotton crop made it over to England, and got top dollar for the cotton. His ship was fired on and sunk on the return trip, but he survived. He let me know that he's bringing our share sometime next week. He decided to pay us even though he lost his ship, since he made enough on the successful trip over to purchase another ship."

Stephen was almost speechless. The thoughts of what to do with that thirty dollars had long ago quit being a subject of speculation for the slaves. They had reckoned that by now, the blockade running had been unsuccessful, and the ship along with their cotton, was resting on the bottom of the ocean.

Miss Annie went on to say, "The Captain of the ship told me that the payment for the cotton would be in gold. This is really good news, as inflation has made the Confederate money almost useless."

Stephen thought, "Thirty dollars in gold is still a real fortune to my mind, and every man, woman and child who remained loyal and kept on working the fields will get to share in the good luck."

Another reason Annie wanted to speak to Stephen was to have him make a census of the remaining field hands. She intended to pay the share of gold which would have gone to the now runaways to the slaves who had remained loyal. She and Stephen went over the list of names and pared it down to those still on the plantation. She calculated that each would receive forty-five dollars, rather than the original agreed-upon thirty. Stephen left the Big House happier than he had been in a long time and he spread the word among the slaves. He guessed he would have no problem with runaways for a time, at least until the field hands received their money.

The big day came, and the field hands lined up to receive their gold and a thank-you from Miss Annie. Stephen was afraid that delivering all of the money into the hands of some of the slaves who were not used to having money might impact the number who would run away. Miss Annie was adamant, in that she wanted to personally deliver the reward at this time to each field hand. She stood in the line until the last of the hands had received his or her reward and she said a personal word of thanks to each for their loyalty and hard work.

Miss Annie also suggested that Stephen warn the slaves that Union General Sherman was known to have come partially through the State of Georgia. He was headed this way, and his men had stolen anything of value from everyone they met and burned most of what could not be moved. She suggested that they find good hiding places for whatever valuables they had, because the slave cabins in Georgia had been searched just like the Big Houses. The same would happen here if the Union army came this way. Stephen took her warnings to heart and passed the information on to the other slaves. After talking to all of the field hands, Stephen guessed to himself there might be as many as eight to ten more runaways now that they had their reward, but he hoped he was wrong.

Stephen and Momma talked about it for some time during the night, and decided they needed to hide their money somewhere that only they knew. They were concerned about both locating a good place and hiding the money undetected.

Stephen finally located an old hollow bee tree, back in the woods not too far from the slave cabins. He put his and Momma's gold coins into an old bandanna, tied it tightly, then slipped it into his shirt. He casually sauntered out into the woods and made several circular walks through the brush and trees to assure that he was not being followed. Eventually, he felt safe and struck out towards the bee tree. He snuck up on the tree, dropped the tied bandanna containing the gold into the hollow, ducked the angry bees which swarmed out, and then ran all the way back to the cabin.

Stephen laughed as he told Momma what he had done, and lowed as how when it came time for them to retrieve the money, they would get a doubly sweet treat. At that time, he would get both gold and honey. He also felt that Sherman's troops, if they arrived on the plantation, would not search for any valuables in that painful spot.

The next day came and life on the plantation went on as usual. The field hands went to the cotton fields to hoe, and Stephen was pleased to find there were only two runaways during the night. Not surprisingly, those two were chronic complainers who really did not carry their weight in the work. The days came and went, as did the rumors of Sherman's progress across Georgia to the southern part of that neighboring state. Stephen and Miss Annie discussed where the valuables in the Big House which still remained unsold could be hidden. They still feared Sherman would change direction and visit South Carolina.

Miss Annie told Stephen, "I give up--I can think of no safe hiding spot. I trust you to find a good place. It would probably be best if as few as possible know about where the silver is hidden, but let me know when you're ready, and I'll collect and wrap what needs to be hidden."

"Yassum," responded Stephen, "I thinks I knows a good hidin place, an I'll probbly jes let Momma heps me, nobody else. Dat stuff ought to be safe, whar I plans to hide it. I waits till nite to hides it so nobuddy sees me."

Rumors continued to fly about Sherman's progress, and the slaves, as well as the whites from the Big House, became more and more concerned. Sherman was known to have crossed into South Carolina, and the plantation was right in the path of the sixty-mile wide scorched earth he was leaving behind him. Stephen went to the Big House late one night, and let Miss Annie know that he was ready to hide the valuables.

Later that night, Stephen reappeared from the Big House, carrying three large, heavy gunny sacks. No one but Miss Annie and her daughters saw him leave. When Miss Annie brought the food and water to the field hands the next day, Stephen gave her a big wink when no one else was looking, and Miss Annie felt a little less concerned about the valuables which would be needed for survival in the event Sherman did burn the plantation; Big House, outbuildings, slave cabins, and everything else would be burned to the ground, judging from what they had heard through the grapevine.

Sherman's path of destruction across the state would weave one way, and the people no longer in his path breathed a little easier. Then, the "dragon" would change directions the next day, and worried faces reappeared. Stephen realized that the cotton in some of the fields was ready to pick. After talking it over with Miss Annie, they decided that it was safer in the fields than in the warehouses on the plantation, which Sherman would undoubtedly burn. Standing cotton was tougher to burn than warehouses. The slaves kept busy by continuing to hoe the ever-voracious weeds and repair broken harness on the plantation. Everyone kept an anxious eye to the west, the direction from which Sherman was expected to come.

Finally, one clear morning, ominous black smoke appeared on

the western horizon, and Stephen realized with a sinking feeling, that the dreaded day was here. He was worried for the white family on the plantation, plus he was worried about what would happen to the slaves. Stories were told about the Yankee monsters selling slaves to the Cubans to work sugar plantations, and the Cubans were said to be even harder masters than Southern whites. Stephen was satisfied with his situation as it currently existed, and he wasn't ready for any drastic changes.

Early one morning, the advance worrying was finally over; a troop of cavalry first appeared as a large dust cloud out on the main road, then turned and rode up the drive to the Big House. The soldiers were all dressed in blue, and Stephen knew the dreaded day was here. The officer in charge of the cavalry unit rode up to the front door. When Miss Annie came out, he brusquely ordered her to immediately assemble all of the slaves on the place. She complied. Thirty minutes later, even the field hands working in the farthest fields had come to the Big House.

The officer turned his back on Miss Annie and rudely ignored her; he addressed only the slaves, and told them, "President Lincoln has declared that slavery is now illegal in this country, and as of now, you're all free men and women. You may stay here if you wish, although there won't be much left when we leave. Or, you may follow us to the sea, and you'll be able to find food and shelter as we move toward Charleston."

When he finished his speech, he was shocked when no expressions was shown on the faces of the newly freed men and women. They made no attempt whatsoever to immediately leave, to follow their "saviors."

He shrugged, and said, "It's your decision—at least stay out of our way while we do our work."

He ordered his men to spread out, and they went in every direction, including into the Big House. Some went toward the slave cabins, and Stephen was momentarily amused to watch one of the soldiers leave his cabin as rapidly as he went in. As he fled, he was pursued by Momma and her broom. Stephen's amusement faded when he saw the soldiers light torches and begin to methodically burn all of the slave cabins to the ground. Momma was forced to leave their home and Stephen cried along with her as they watched the only home Stephen had ever known turn into a smoldering pile of ashes. The soldiers next burned all of the barns.

The captain went up to Miss Annie and said in a curt voice, "It will go better for you if you tell me now, where you've hidden the silver and other valuables. We'll find them anyway, and I can't promise that some of my men won't get rough, if you don't talk."

Stephen took a deep breath, then walked over to Miss Annie and her daughters, and told the captain, "Suh, please don talk tuh Miss Annie like dat. She has been a good mistress, and we all lubs her jes lik we lubs our own mommas. Lebs her alone."

To the captain's surprise, as well as to Stephen's, the majority of the ex-slaves, even though now free men and women, joined Stephen in a protective ring around Miss Annie and her daughters.

"All right, we'll find it ourselves!" angrily shouted the captain, and the soldiers began searching the plantation again, looking for telltale signs of fresh earth, or other evidence of attempts to hide the valuables. If a slave stood in the way of the search, the soldiers simply pushed them away and several were swatted with rifle butts, leaving bloodied heads.

Several soldiers discovered the gold chalice, candlesticks, and paten in the small chapel next to the Big House. It had been so long since an Episcopal priest had managed to come to the plantation to celebrate service, that Miss Annie had frankly forgotten the presence of the gold items, inherited from her family as far back as before they first left England. Sadly, even those sacred items found their way into the seemingly bottomless gunny sacks which the soldiers carried. The soldiers also found in the now-cooling ashes, a few pieces of the gold which some of the slaves had left in their cabins instead of successfully hiding them. No amount of crying and pleading that it was the ex-slaves' money forced the soldiers to return it.

The soldiers became more and more angry as their search for

the valuables from the Big House remained fruitless, until the captain gave up. He ordered the men to torch the Big House, then ordered his men to gather up the livestock, but shoot those animals not in the best of shape. Sporadic rifle shots were heard around the plantation. The troops moved out, driving the majority of the animals ahead of them. They left, as promised, very few stones on top of one another, and most of the plantation was burned or was smoldering.

The ex-slaves hurriedly formed a bucket brigade, and saved most of the back portion of the Big House. Tired, smoky, and with burns on both hands, Stephen walked over to Miss Annie, and tried to comfort her.

"Dat's allrite, Miss Annie, dey didn find de good stuff, and dat will come in handy later. Fer now, we best git goin on buildin some shelter afore night come."

"Stephen," said Miss Annie, "We'll do that, but first, I would appreciate it if you would please call the other servants over here."

He sent out the word and five minutes later, Miss Annie stood to talk to them.

"I appreciate how all of you have remained faithful to me, even though you've had many chances to run away over this last year. As you heard from that Yankee officer, you're now all free, and you may leave if you so choose. For those of you who decide to remain here and work on the plantation; I can't pay much, but we'll work out some small amount of pay as I am able."

She stopped, and stepped back to watch. She was pleased that only five of the men and two of their women decided to leave. These individuals packed what few clothes they were able to save before their cabins were destroyed and left the plantation. They headed for Charleston and they hoped, a new and better, free life.

Miss Annie sent the hands around the plantation to collect the animals Sherman's men had massacred, and they had a feast later that night, even though the animals butchered were of the older, tougher variety. The addition of meat to their diet for the first time in weeks gave everyone new strength. The servants gathered around Stephen after dinner to talk about what had to be done next, to provide shelter. All the now freed men and women who remained on the plantation began collecting what boards and bricks they could salvage, and small shelters were constructed. A new wall was built to separate the burned from the unburned portions of the house to make part of the Big House livable again.

Miss Annie went over to Stephen and in a whisper told him, "Stephen, I don't know how you managed to hide the silver and valuables so those vultures didn't spot them, but I owe you thanks again. I seem to spend a lot of my time thanking you for assistance."

"Dat's all right, Miss Annie," responded Stephen. "I hid it good, dat's fer sho. Dem bluebellies ain't as smart as dey tink dey am. Meybe we bes leave it hidden for some time, till we sho dere no dittional vultures."

He resumed directing the work efforts, and before nightfall, Miss Annie and the girls were safely tucked away in a small shack, away from the cold, damp night air. Most of the slaves slept that night in the shelter of trees or bushes. The efforts to do what they could to resurrect the plantation to a livable condition continued for the next few weeks.

Miss Annie sought out Stephen one morning. She asked, "Can you reclaim the smallest of the three gunny sacks of valuables? I've found a buyer for part of the silver, and I'll use that money for lumber and perhaps a few animals, if we can find any for sale around the countryside."

"Yassum," replied Stephen, and to her surprise, he went over to the former pigpen, and began digging into the sloppy mud. He reappeared, covered with smelly mud, but he was carrying the sack she had requested. Stephen told her, "Miss Annie, dat's why I got de sacks several days fore dem Yankees came. I figgered dat de pigs would wallow ober de digging and hide it, sos dem Yankees wouldn't see dat dere had been diggin goin on. Ebben though dey killed or stole all de pigs, de pigs did their work. All de stuff be safe."

Miss Annie laughed, for the first time in many weeks. "Stephen, you're a gem. I never would have thought of that. I believe we'll be all right, and we should be able to somehow get this plantation into some semblance of what it was like, maybe even before Young Will comes back from the war. This place will never be quite what it was, but I hope we can be proud of what it becomes."

Stephen nodded his agreement, and led the field hands out into the cotton field for the first time in several weeks. Life went on, alternating between picking and construction. For the field hands, differentiation between freedom and slavery was a tough task that, for now, maybe took too much time from other things that had to be done. Maybe later it would all sink in.

☐ ☐ ☐ ☐

CHAPTER SEVENTEEN
THE LAST LEGS
Nathan
Spring, 1865

The war was tottering on its last legs. The once-great Southern armies were almost decimated. The Army of Northern Virginia, including the Holcombe Legion with which Will and Nathan served, was the last with any hopes of success. Even those hopes were dim, to the point of non-existent. Around the campfires each evening, the singing which for four years had been one of the highlights of the day, either did not occur at all, or the songs that were sung by the men were so sad that their depression deepened, rather than improved.

Will told Nathan late one day after the daily officers' meeting, the Confederacy was considering putting slaves into uniform and arming them to bolster its ranks. However, the powers that be were not really considering it very seriously. Nathan's eyes got a little wider for a moment as he thought about that hopefully remote possibility.

Nathan came back down to earth and went to fix dinner. Even though some of the servants he knew had occasionally picked up a weapon during a battle and killed a few Yankees, he wasn't sure but what being a body servant was somewhat better than being an actual soldier.

At least during the heat of the battles and skirmishes, Nathan and the other servants sat out the action as far to the rear as they could get, and the bullets seldom flew in their direction. That was far better then being on the front ranks. Nathan was glad that nothing was mentioned again about this unlikely idea. He felt that his loyalty was to Captain Will and the other men of the Holcombe Legion, and not really to the Confederacy, and he was pleased that the threat to arm the ex-slaves was never carried out.

Dinner, such as it was, was interrupted by the sudden sounds of nearby battle, and the pickets for the Holcombe Legion were unexpectedly engaged with scout cavalry troops from Sherman's Army who thought they would find little resistance in their sweep through South Carolina. After ten minutes of skirmishing, the northern cavalry retreated and rode back south to rejoin the main body of Sherman's raiders.

The officers of the Legion and the other units in the area came together in haste and agreed to immediately move further north and try to rally the other Confederate troops that were rumored to be there. The Legion packed their pittance of supplies and moved out in the moonlight. They rode most of the night and all of the next day in a quiet daze and they stopped and encamped just south of the boundary between South and North Carolina.

The exhausted troops and officers went to sleep after posting guards. Most did not bother to set up tents, but collapsed where they were, Nathan included. With the exception of the guards, it is doubtful that any member of the Legion stirred at all the entire night. It was a good thing that Sherman and his hordes did not come that night, because the truth is, many of the guards slept also, an action punishable by death earlier in the war. There were too few men to consider such a punishment now.

Nothing transpired during the night and the men began waking up at eight o'clock the next morning. The officers held another meeting, as all involved realized that the hoped-for support troops were non-existent; the Holcombe Legion was on its own. The officers discussed what they should do next, and decided to move on up into North Carolina and find the best possible place to dig in for their last stand.

After a quick breakfast, the Legion marched most of that day. There were no bands or drums and few flags to stir the patriotism in any man's breast. The ragged, dirty, and shoeless men stumbled mostly; the word march is an untrue glorification. But, somehow, they kept moving.

They found a location where the soldiers could command the top of a slope leading down to a large stream, and defense would be good. The troops dug in and cut a few large trees as a redoubt and as temporary breastworks. They lay on their arms and waited for the inevitable appearance of the pursuing Northern troops. Their attitudes were of resignation and finality.

Nathan, as was his custom, went to the rear and stood by the supply wagons. He noticed that what few supply wagons were left held almost no supplies and no food. He concluded that their part of the war was almost over. When you have no food, you will be able to fight on for a little while, but when you have no ammunition or powder, your fighting days are limited.

Nathan and the others waited in vain for sounds of battle, but except for a few scattered sniper shots, the anticipated last-gasp battle never began. The news of General Robert E. Lee's surrender up in Appomatox, Virginia, swept over the armies of both North and South during the evening. All realized that the last shots had been fired in this part of the action and the war was over for them.

Nathan wasn't sure whether to be happy or sad, but the majority of the white soldiers felt that their world had come to a screeching halt. This was an accurate interpretation, because in reality, their world as it had existed prior to 1860, had just collapsed. What they would do next and what would happen to them, was paramount on all minds, black and white alike. Most had a mixed reaction to the end of the past four years. Glad they had survived; glad the marching and living in the weather on poor or no rations was over. Sad that the glorious effort to self-govern, as most of the whites believed the war was about, had been defeated. Sad that the hated Yankees now had complete power over them, both in the present and in the future.

The next few days were a blur for all of the men of the Legion, as they lay down their arms and were placed under arrest by the Union forces. The mental attitude of the defeated officers and men were as low as humanly possible. The morale of the body servants, the few which were still serving the Legion, was no better, as they felt the defeat just as bitterly as did the combatants.

The census and pardon process which had been agreed upon by Lee and Grant at Appomatox took about a week to set into place, but finally it was completed. Nathan prepared to depart, to accompany Will back home to South Carolina. The Yankees worked hard on Nathan and the other ex-slaves trying to convince them that as they were now free, they did not have to accompany their ex-masters and they could go where they wanted.

Nathan drew himself up to his full height and announced to the officer talking to him that, "Ize already free, and since Ize free, I'll gwine whar I want tuh gwine. I goes wit Will. Ize gwine home to see my Momma and my brudder an I plans to stay rite dere."

The Union officer finally left him alone, shaking his head with a complete lack of understanding.

As Will and Nathan prepared to go home, the two men surveyed their available supplies and equipment. The pardoning process allowed Will to keep his sidearm and his horses, so at least they would not have to walk and they would have some protection from the scavengers which were all over the virtually-destroyed countryside. Their tattered tents were packed and would give a little bit of protection against the night dew. Nathan and Will completed their packing, and started their trek.

Will did not say much; Nathan did not push him, realizing that the past few weeks had been hard on a proud son of the South. They made their way down through southern North Carolina, and into South Carolina.

Nathan and Will were appalled at the complete devastation they saw along the way. Sherman's troops had been extremely zealous in their attempts to extract revenge on the area where the rebellion had first started some four years ago. Sherman was successful in attaining complete devastation. Food was almost impossible to come by, and the two men, like everyone else in the area, had to forage near and far to find anything at all to eat.

On the second night of their trip, Nathan and Will had eaten their tiny portion of food and lay down and slept. At about two o'clock in the morning, a small noise woke Nathan. He crept out of his tent and saw three Negroes on the opposite side of the campfire coals, going through their few supplies. He shouted and the three men started for him, with clubs raised. Nathan figured that he was in real trouble; he picked up a fire log, and got ready to defend himself.

Just then, Will's quiet voice came from the entrance of his tent, "If you touch that man, this revolver is going to extract immediate retribution. Are you all prepared to die right here and now?"

The three scavengers stopped in their tracks.

One of the men stepped forward, and said, "We ain't had nuttin tuh eat for two or three days. Iffin we don't git someting, our families are gwine starve. Dat's why we wuz pokin thru you stuff."

Will came out of his tent, and walked over to the men, watching them warily. He wanted to do the right thing, but he still clutched his revolver, in case further trouble came. "We'll share what we have, some beans and a little cornmeal. Maybe that'll be enough to feed you for a couple of days, but that's all we have. We don't know what kind of shape our own families are in, as Sherman came through our home as well."

Will motioned for Nathan to divide the food evenly, while he continued to watch the men.

"Tank you," said the ringleader of the three men. "Dis will make a few meals, an now my babies mebbe not cry all de time. The Yankees has set up a food center fer new freemen obber in de next county, an I reckon we has tuh gwine obber dere tuh git eny food. We won't bodder you enny more."

The near-starved scavengers walked away, and Will and Nathan both breathed huge sighs of relief.

The next morning followed extremely restless sleep, as the two alternated with guard duty. Nathan and Will packed up and rode further south, dreading what they would find as they arrived at the once-proud plantation in the Low Country. Will was a little more talkative this morning and he told Nathan he figured they would arrive home in two or three more hard days of riding and that they wouldn't tarry. Safety was obviously going to be a problem. The men took turns watching the road before and behind them to make sure no one would be able to slip up on them.

The trip passed with no further violent incidents, although they were accosted many times every day by people begging food. Nathan and Will shared what little they had left. For the last day and a half, the two men had no food at all for themselves, and their bellies loudly protested.

As they rode into their home county, the signs of devastation did not diminish, as virtually every plantation they rode by had been burned, and most appeared to be deserted, except for an occasional barking dog. The dogs showed their treatment and lack of food, and ribs were evident on the few animals they saw. Livestock was nonexistent. The winds of war had definitely blown hard and cold on South Carolina, and their home state had paid dearly for the sins of the Confederacy, at least as those sins existed in Northern eyes.

CHAPTER EIGHTEEN
HOME, SWEET(?), HOME
Nathan and Stephen
Spring, 1865

Will and Nathan slowly rode over the last rise, and gasped as they first laid eyes on the wreck of the plantation. They could see the remnants of the Big House and where the other buildings and barns had stood and burned wood was everywhere. The few remaining hunting dogs spotted them and began barking. The two men rode closer. Will's Mother, dressed in field hand clothes, emerged from the front door of a shack under one of the few palmetto trees which had survived the fires.

"Will," she cried, and he jumped off his horse and ran to her and his sisters and enveloped all of them in a hug.

"It appears that General Sherman and his friends have been here with a vengeance," observed Will as he looked around at the destruction.

"He has, indeed, but we have some good news," responded Miss Annie. "Thanks to my foreman, Stephen, we were able to save virtually all of the silver which has been in the family for over a hundred years, and that'll help us get this plantation back on its feet. I think our relatives will smile down on us as we use their legacy to do that."

As this discussion was taking place, another reunion was occurring. Stephen and Momma had spotted the tall, slim black man with Will, but they hadn't recognized him at first. Once they realized who it was, they practically pulled him off of his horse, crying and laughing at the same time as they smothered Nathan with hugs.

"Little brudder, I hears dat you dun well round dis place," Nathan told Stephen.

"Didn't do nuttin dat you wouldn't hab dun," responded Stephen. "Oh, Nathan, I wants you to meets sumbody. Here she am." Stephen drug Cassie by the arm to stand in front of Nathan.

Nathan said, "Little bruder, I knows Cassie--she dun libs nex to us since she was born."

Stephen replied, "Yes, but she now be my wife. We be married las year."

Nathan stood there with his mouth open for a minute, then grinned and reached to hug Cassie. "Welcome, Cassie, Ize happy fer you two. Anyway, Stephen, Ize proud ob you fer what you dun whiles Ize gone," Nathan said. "Now, what does me an Mister Will needs tuh git dun round here?"

Stephen immediately passed on tasks for Nathan and Will. Both men laughed at the new authoritarian Stephen, and began work. They helped to clear rubble and with construction, working on both tasks at the same time.

Nathan had to stop and speak with the remaining hands, most of whom he had known since his birth. Old Ned spotted Nathan, and greeted him with a huge hug.

Nathan told him, "Ned, Ize proud youze still here--you dun been lik my daddy, an it wouldn't be de same iffen you wuz not here."

"Got no---whar else to go---dese fo---o---o---ks am my famb---b---ly an dis be my ho---o---me. Glad youze ba---c---k, Nat---t---than."

The following months sped by with the hectic schedule. Nathan became more and more restless and morose, as he wondered what happened to Sadie. Nobody at his plantation knew anything at all about her whereabouts.

Will finally said to Nathan one day, "All right Nathan, if you're going to moon around here like a sick calf, we might as well go ahead and try to find Sadie. Why don't you get your gear together, and we'll go next door, and see if we can find her."

Nathan needed no additional prompting and he ran to saddle both horses. The two men mounted and started toward the plantation, several miles away. They did not say much during the ride, but both groaned when they came out of the woods that surrounded that plantation. It was in worse shape than their own; only no work had been done to try to repair the buildings or make them livable. They scouted around, but found no people, and certainly no clues as to what might have happened to Sadie or any of the other residents of the now destroyed plantation.

Nathan said to Will, "Ize powerful unhappy. I don knows whar she be, an we can't finds out nuttin."

Will told Nathan, "Don't give up so easy. We'll keep hunting, maybe ride on to the next plantation, and see if we can get some information."

The two mounted and rode to the next place.

As they approached the remnant of the house, dogs started barking. Nathan and Will looked at one another, and felt a bit of encouragement. They halloed the house, and the owner came out onto the porch.

"Will," exclaimed the man. "Good to see you! We'd heard that some work was going on at your place, and we were hoping that you'd survived that dreadful war."

Will dismounted and the two shook hands. "Here is one reason I survived the war," said Will. "This is Nathan, a freeman, who served me valiantly during those four years and saved me a number of times. He and his family are living and working with us."

"Pleased to meet you, Nathan," said the man. "Now, what can I do for you men?" he asked.

"We're looking for someone," said Will. "A woman that used to be a slave. Her name is Sadie and she lived over on the plantation between you and me. Have you any information about where any of the folks from next door are?"

The man scratched his chin for a moment and pondered the question. "I don't hardly know where they might be. I believe that some of the nigras from next door might be living bout three miles from here, down by the river. They have a shanty town down there, and I don't know for a fact, but it's possible that she might be there. You might at least get some information."

"Thanks very much," said Will, "We'll try down there."

"You'd best be careful," said the man. "I understand they don't cotton to white men down there very much."

"We'll be careful. Thanks again."

Nathan and Will again mounted, and moved on.

The men rode for about an hour, searching up and down the river bank. A very large, frowning black man suddenly stepped from behind a tree and pointed a businesslike rifle in their direction.

"What's you wants down here, white man?" asked the man. "An for dat matter, what you doin wid him, nigger?"

Nathan replied, "You kin put dat gun down, man. We is jes lookin fer sumbudy, a woman who was a slave on de Jones plantation. Do you knows a woman named Sadie?"

The question hung in the air between questioner and questioned.

"Reckon I mite," finally responded the man. "What's you wants wid her?"

"I wants to talk wid her," said Nathan. "Dat's all. She be a friend of mine. I ain't seed her for sebbral years."

The man thought deeply for a moment, then said, "I reckon it am alrite. De onliest reason I paused is cause my woman has kinda took Sadie on as her own, after our daughter died durin de war. She is mitey kerful bout who she lets talk wid her. Come on, dey be down dis way."

The man led them down a narrow path, and they entered the shanty town, perched precariously on the bank of the river. When the inhabitants saw the visitors, Will was surrounded by a circle of angry black men, several carrying clubs and guns. They were not a very pleasant greeting committee.

"Wait," said their guide. "Dese men be alrite. Dey wants to talk wid Miz Sadie, dat's all. Leave em be."

The men reluctantly parted the circle and allowed Will some breathing room. Sadie came out of a shack to find out what all the ruckus was.

"Nathan," she proclaimed. "I didn't think you wuz still alive! I shore be glad to see you!"

She gave him a big hug, which Nathan returned with interest. The man who first accosted Will and Nathan grinned from ear to ear. The happy reunion came to a halt and the grin disappeared, when Sadie's foster momma came out of the shack.

"Sadie," she exclaimed. "Turn loose of dat nigger an gits back inside. Sam, you gits dat grin plumb offen you face, afore I removes it permanent-like."

Sadie stepped back, and explained, "Momma Pearl, dis here am Nathan, de man I telled you about. I knowed him befo de war. He has come back safe and sound and I am tickled to death to sees him. Be nice, he am a good man."

Pearl removed some of the scowl from her face, but was a long way from being fully convinced. "Whether he am a good man or no am still a question fer me. He haz to proves it, yet."

Nathan and Will looked at one another, and felt a little less uneasy.

Pearl, perhaps with a bit of remorse for her earlier attack, said, "We ain't gots much, but you-uns welcome to share it. I got sum beans and hamhock an some collard greens ready to eat. I believe de cornbread ought be dun in dat oven. Checks it fer me," she brusquely ordered Nathan.

Nathan hurried to comply. "Yessum, I do jes dat," he said over his shoulder as he moved toward the outdoor oven. He carefully opened the door, and sniffed the aroma with a connoisseur's nose and said, "It shore look perfect to me, mighty near as purty as me or my Momma make."

"Bring it ober here den, an let's eat," Pearl again ordered.

Pearl, Sam, Nathan, Sadie, and Will ate until they could eat no more.

"That was mighty good," exclaimed Will. "Best meal I've had in months. We're obliged for you feeding us."

"You am welcom," said Pearl. "I believe dat Nathan mite be a good man after all. Eny man eat dat much of my cookin be all rite. What am you intentions, Nathan?" She had suddenly changed tactics, keeping Nathan off balance.

Nathan gulped, then replied to Pearl, "I telled Sadie durin de war dat I wants her to marry me an I still wants dat, iffen she haz me."

Pearl stopped him with a withering look. "I tink it mite be nice were you to ask her, not me. Ize already married."

Nathan turned to Sadie, and asked, "Sadie, will you marry me? I haz a good home, and I plans to grow cotton and corn an . . . "

Sadie interrupted, "Of course I will. It's bout time you come back to ask me. I bin waitin fer seems like years now, an Ize bout waited out."

Nathan's head felt giddy, much like when he got the rifle butt to the head back in Charleston, only now it was a pleasant pain, rather than a splitting headache.

"Well then, it's settled," said Will. "I can get the priest to come down to the plantation within the next few weeks. All of you are invited to the wedding. I'll let you know when we can arrange for the priest to visit."

Good-byes were said all around, and Will rode and Nathan floated, as they returned home.

Over the next several months, many scroungers and would-be villains approached people on the plantation. As they were confronted by white and black men and women steadily holding firearms, the word soon spread that that particular plantation was a good place to avoid. The appearances of unwanted people trickled to near zero.

One day, Will walked over to the barn where Nathan and Stephen were working and called them down from the ladders on which the two men were perched.

"I need to talk with you two for a bit," started Will, as the three sat in the shade which was slightly cooler than on the ladders: a nice breeze helped somewhat. "Both of you, although in very different circumstances, helped my family in ways which we can never repay. Nathan, you saved my arm, and maybe even my life on several occasions. Now, you're about to have a new wife, and you need a better home than the shed where you're living. Stephen, after talking to my mother, you did the same for her, and you certainly saved the remnants of the family money.

Again, we believe that thanks aren't sufficient, but we have an idea which might show our appreciation in a small way. You two, like everyone else who was a slave on this plantation, are of course now free men. Property ownership for freed slaves is still up in the air in the South, but Mother and I've decided to do with our land as we wish. We will worry about the legalities when we must. We've decided to give the two of you one hundred acres of land, down on the southern boundary of this plantation. The river flows by the west part of that land, and we believe you'll be able to build a nice place for yourselves and your Momma down there. There are plenty of forests and the soil is excellent for whatever crops you might plant. We hope you'll continue to help us rebuild our place, but we'll understand if you don't have as much time as you did have."

Nathan and Stephen were speechless. They stammered out thanks, but Will was amply rewarded by the broad grins which appeared on their faces and on Momma's face when they rushed over to tell her the news.

After the initial shock of the news had worn off, Nathan and Stephen went down to the property, accompanied by Momma and Will. They excitedly planned the location of the future house and what needed to be done first. Stephen proudly told of his gold, earned by the successful blockade running late in the war. Nathan also had his cache of gold from his sock washing business and the money he had earned as a paid servant. Between them, they figured they had a good start on buying building material for their new house.

Nathan, thinking aloud, stated, "I reckon dat dis be sufficient to buy a little bit of lumber, least enough to git started. We has to keep on workin for Mister Will to earn enuff money to keep on buildin."

Will breathed a sigh of relief. "I was hoping that would be your plan—we'd be hard pressed to do without the two of you."

The three men, as employer and employees and land-owners and planters, along with a strangely quiet and pensive Momma, rode back to the remnants of the Big House. An era in their lives, as well as in the lives of a still-young nation, had come to a close. It might be almost one hundred years from that time when Nathan and Stephen's relatives would be truly free and feel that way, but the first huge chasm had been bridged, albeit by the blood and lives of many men, Northern and Southern alike. They were free and Nathan, Stephen and their Momma were now property owners; that was one of the results of four years of conflict. That was all they knew at that time; that was sufficient.

☐ ☐ ☐ ☐

GLOSSARY

WORD	DIALECT
afraid	fraid
allegiance	'legiance
altogether	altogeder
always	allus
ambulance	"amulet, or omlet"
and	an'
Apostle	'Postle
appear	pear
at all	a tall
before	'fore
Bless	Bress
breath	bref
brother	brudder
can	kin
care	keer
careful	keerful
carried	toted
certain sure	sartin
child	chile
children	chilen
claim	clam
clear	clar
cloak	cloke
Colonel	Cunnel
colored	cullud
come	cum
condensed milk	condemned milk
correct	correck
curse	cuss
daughter	darter
despise	'spise
destruction	'struction
devil	debbil
dollar	dollah

WORD	DIALECT
done	dun
drop	drap
early A.M.	'fore coffees' hot
ever	eber
every	ebry
except	perceps
excepting	inception
expect	spec'
fighter	fightingest
first	"fus', or dus'"
First South Carolina	Fus' Souf
first thing	fus'ting
generally	ginerally
gentleman	gemman
gird on the armor	guide on the army
give	gib
go	gwine
going	gwine
going to	gwine
government	guv'ment
guard duty	guard-mountin'
have	hab
heaven	heaben
himself	heseff
his	he
horse	hoss
I will	Ise
I would	I'ud
if	iffen
impressment officer	"'pressin' agent; or, conscrip's"
in (into)	e'en
it	hit
jubilee	jubilo
just	jess

WORD	DIALECT
just about	jist er bout
land	lan'
left	lef'
like	lak
Lincoln	Linkum
live	lib
Lord	Lor
love	lub
loved	lubed
loyal heart	colored-man heart
Master	"Mas'r; or, Massa"
Mistress	Mist'ess
mother	mudder
never	neber
next	nex'
nothing	notin'
obliged	'bleeged
of	ob
old	ole
other	oder
out of	o'
person	pusson
poor white person	Cracker or Buckra
preserved	'served
pretty	purty
repent	'pent
scared	skerred
Secesionist	Secesh
seven	seben
Sir	Sah
soldier	sojer
something	somfin'
spirit	sperrit
stand	stan'
suppose	s'pose

WORD	DIALECT
sure	sho'
take	tek
terrible	turrble
that	dat
that's	da's
the	de
their	dem
them	"'em, or dey, or dem"
then	den
there	"dere, or dar"
thing	ting
think	a-tink
think them	tink 'em
thinking	a-tinking
this	dis
three	tree
through	troo
thrown	chucked
thy	dy
to	tuh
to hoe	a hoein'
trust	truss
very	berry
was	wuz
what for?	wof for?
where is	whar's
whip	whup
whippoorwill	Chuckwill's widow
white man	buckra
with	wid
without	widout
work	wuck
"Yes, Sir"	Yas Sar
your	yer

BIBLIOGRAPHY

Glatthaar, Joseph, 1990: *Forged in Battle: The Civil War Alliance of Black Soldiers and White Officers.*, 1990: The Free Press, McMillan, Inc., New York, New York.

Glatthaar, Joseph, 1992: *Black Glory: The African-American Role in Union Victory.* In: *Why the Confederacy Lost*, 1992: Gabor S. Boritt, Oxford University Press, New York, New York.

Gooding, Corporal James Henry, 1991: *On the Altar of Freedom: A Black Soldier's Civil War Letters From the Front.* The University of Massachusetts Press, Amherst, Massachusetts, 139 pp.

Gordon, Asa H., 1929: *Sketches of Negro Life and History in South Carolina.* The University of South Carolina Press, Columbia, South Carolina.

Higginson, Thomas Wentworth, 1870: *Army Life in a Black Regiment.* Fields, Osgood and Company, Boston, Massachusetts.

Litwack, Leon F., 1870: *Been in the Storm So Long: The Aftermath of Slavery.* Alfred A. Knopf Publishing, New York, New York.

McPherson, James M., 1965: *The Negro's Civil War.* Pantheon Books, A Division of Random House, New York, New York.

Newton, A.H., D.D., 1910: *Out of the Briars.* Mnemosyne Publishing Co. (republished in 1969), Miami, Florida.

Quarles, Benjamin, 1953: *The Negro in the Civil War.* Little, Brown and Company, Boston, Massachusetts.

Roark, James L., 1977: *Masters Without Slaves.*
W.W.Norton and Company, Ltd., Toronto, Canada.

Wiley, Bell Irvin, 1938: *Southern Negroes, 1861-1865.*
Louisiana State University Press, Baton Rouge, Louisiana.

Williamson, Joel, 1965: *After Slavery: The Negro in South Carolina During Reconstruction, 1861-1877.*
W.W.Norton & Company, Inc., New York, New York.

Wilkinson, Warren, 1990: Mother, May You Never See the Sights I Have Seen: The Fifty-Seventh Massachusetts Veteran Volunteers in the Army of the Potomac, 1864-1865. Harper & Row, Publishers, New York, New York.

ORDER FORM

Postal Orders: Paint Rock Publishing, Inc.
                          118 Dupont Smith Lane
                          Kingston, TN 37763
                          (423) 376-3892

Please Send the Following Books:
(I understand that I may return any book
for a full refund—for any reason, no questions)

                                              Price: _____
                                              Price: _____
                                              Price: _____

Sales Tax: Please add 7.5% for books shipped to Tennessee addresses.

                                                Tax: _____

Shipping:
Book Rate: $3.00 for first book and
.75 cents for each additional book
(shipping may take three weeks)
Air Mail: $4.50 per book.

                                          Shipping: _____

Payment: Check or money order.
Do not send cash.

                                                Total: _____

ORDER NOW——THANK YOU

ORDER FORM

Postal Orders: Paint Rock Publishing, Inc.
                 118 Dupont Smith Lane
                 Kingston, TN 37763
                 (423) 376-3892

Please Send the Following Books:
(I understand that I may return any book
for a full refund—for any reason, no questions)

                                              Price: _____

                                              Price: _____

                                              Price: _____

Sales Tax: Please add 7.5% for books shipped to Tennessee addresses.

                                              Tax: _____

Shipping:
Book Rate: $3.00 for first book and .75 cents for each additional book (shipping may take three weeks)
Air Mail: $4.50 per book.

                                        Shipping: _____

Payment: Check or money order. Do not send cash.

                                              Total: _____

ORDER NOW——THANK YOU

ORDER FORM

Postal Orders: Paint Rock Publishing, Inc.
                 118 Dupont Smith Lane
                 Kingston, TN 37763
                 (423) 376-3892

Please Send the Following Books:
(I understand that I may return any book
for a full refund—for any reason, no questions)

                                                  Price: _____

                                                  Price: _____

                                                  Price: _____

Sales Tax: Please add 7.5% for books
shipped to Tennessee addresses.

                                                  Tax: _____

Shipping:
Book Rate: $3.00 for first book and
.75 cents for each additional book
(shipping may take three weeks)
Air Mail: $4.50 per book.

                                        Shipping: _____

Payment: Check or money order.
Do not send cash.

                                                  Total: _____

ORDER NOW——THANK YOU